HAPPY HUNTING GROUNDS

HAPPY HUNTING GROUNDS

By Stanley Vestal
Introduction by Peter J. Powell
Illustrated by Frederick Weygold

University of Oklahoma Press
Norman

Books by Stanley Vestal (Walter S. Campbell) published by the
University of Oklahoma Press
The Booklovers Southwest
Sitting Bull, Champion of the Sioux: A Biography
Happy Hunting Grounds

Library of Congress Catalog Card Number 71-5134

ISBN: 978-0-8061-1543-6 (paper)

The paper in this book meets the guidelines for permanence and durability of
the Committee on Production Guidelines for Book Longevity of the Council
Library Resources, Inc.

In Memory of
MY MOTHER

Stanley Vestal
(Walter S. Campbell)
Courtesy Western History Collections
University of Oklahoma Libraries

INTRODUCTION
By Peter J. Powell

Supernatural beauty and harsh reality mingled to form the essence of traditional Plains Indian life. Few non-Indians comprehend this fact, especially in these days when so much romanticizing appears under the guise of Plains Indian history. Fewer still are those non-Indians possessing sufficient firsthand knowledge and literary skill to portray Plains Indian life accurately, so that others may themselves glimpse the nature of that life where harshness mingled with beauty, Happily, one man accomplished both feats in this single volume.

Happy Hunting Grounds was Stanley Vestal's (Walter S. Campbell's) third book. It was, however, his first Indian volume, preceding his now-definitive biography of Sitting Bull by some four years. Yet, because it was published as a novel for young people, *Happy Hunting Grounds* has remained all but unnoticed since appearing in 1928. At that point the author was a mature man of forty-one years. He was also professor of English in the University of Oklahoma. He already had distinguished himself as the first Rhodes Scholar from the new state of Oklahoma, graduating from Oxford University with honors in both English language and literature.

Walter Stanley Campbell was born in Fredonia, Kansas, in 1887. His father, Walter M. Vestal, died soon after the son's birth. The young man would preserve that father's memory in the pen name of Stanley Vestal, the name under which most of his major works appeared. His mother became a teacher, "a profession she followed with enthusiasm for much of her life," Walter once wrote. She also led him to read good literature. Later she would remarry, Walter's stepfather being J. R. Campbell, first president of Southwestern State Normal School at Weatherford, Oklahoma. "My stepfather had been one of Bancroft's men and the history of the West was a familiar subject in the family," Walter Campbell later recalled.[1] Thus fine literary taste and an intense interest in the West were imbued in him at an early age.

[1] Stanley J. Kunitz and Howard Haycraft, editors, *Twentieth Century Authors* (New York H. W. Wilson and Company, 1942), 241f.

Introduction

Weatherford was close to the Southern Cheyenne lands, and it was the Cheyennes who first instilled in Walter Campbell a love for the Plains tribes, a love that remained undiminished throughout his lifetime. His Southern Cheyenne teachers were distinguished men: George Bent, son of William Bent of Bent's Fort, and Owl Woman, daughter of White Thunder, Keeper of the Sacred Arrows; Thunder Bull and Burnt All Over, old-time fighting men; Felix Roman Nose, son of Chief Roman Nose Thunder, a younger man who nevertheless held fast to the old Cheyenne sacred ways; and finally, Hubbell Big Horse, an artist whose Cheyenne battle scenes are today among the major glories of the Field Museum of Natural History in Chicago.

Later, as Walter Campbell researched and recorded the lives of Sitting Bull and White Bull, he would treasure the friendship of many old-time Northern Cheyenne and Teton Lakota warriors. However, it was from the Southern Cheyennes that the inspiration for *Happy Hunting Grounds* sprang. This debt of gratitude he acknowledged in the first two paragraphs of his foreword, certainly one of the finest and most personal tributes ever accorded a people by one outside of them.

In many ways this is the most personal of Walter Campbell's volumes. His love of the Plains tribes and of their country radiates from every page, and its characters are animated by the personalities of actual figures in Plains Indian history. For example, in his characterization of Ironshirt, he draws upon his knowledge of Roman Nose, the great Cheyenne warrior who moved in battle as rapidly as a bat in flight. This was the Roman Nose who wore Thunder's own warbonnet, a warbonnet whose supernatural power could be broken only by eating food touched by an iron spoon. Roman Nose, like Ironshirt, inadvertently ate such food. Then, like Ironshirt, he rode out to certain death in battle.

Whirlwind, the central figure in *Happy Hunting Grounds*, suffers the tragic loss of his son, but publicly refuses to acknowledge the boy's death. In Walter Campbell's characterization of the Cheyenne chief's love for his son, he draws upon the actions of the Kiowa chief Sitting Bear following the death of Sitting Bear's best-beloved son.

And there are lesser characters whose actions originated in Campbell's intimate knowledge of Plains Indian life. Chief among them is the aged mother of Whirlwind, a woman whose grief is so terrible that she tears away the film covering her blind old eyes. Her prototype was a venerable Cheyenne woman, known by the young Stanley Vestal, a woman whom he once described as being the bravest person he ever had known.

There are minor historical and ethnological errors in this work. These will be readily apparent to any serious student of Plains Indian life. However, these errors seem unimportant when contrasted to what Walter Campbell accomplished in the creation of this novel. As I re-read it now, more than thirty years after I first devoured its contents, I am struck anew by the power of the writing. One assumes that he, the professor of English, would possess competent literary skills. Here, however, he is much more than competent. In *Happy Hunting Grounds* there is a richness of description surpassing that found in any of his other volumes. And here, more than anywhere else, Walter Campbell demonstrates a unique ability to recapture the vitality, the harshness, and the supernatural beauty that intermingled to form traditional Plains Indian life. The profound holiness of the Hunka ceremony, the poetry of color and motion formed by warriors clashing in battle, the vitality of a Cheyenne camp on the move; the awesome natural splendor surrounding the Blackfeet as they camped in the Rockies—all live once more in these pages. And no words have better captured the mood of a feast for the dead than does this one sentence:

So the feasters, wrapped in their white robes, left the painted tipi noiselessly, and slipped away through the gray dawn like ghosts, while a malformed moon, red and ugly, quite killed the white beauty of the morning star.

It was the sunset of old-time Cheyenne life that filled young Walter Stanley Campbell's eyes as he raced his uncle's ponies up the North Canadian. Fortunately, when he became a man, he could not bring himself to put away the memory of what he had both seen and heard there. *Happy Hunting Grounds* recaptures life when the Cheyenne Sun was at its zenith. It was a life at once sacred and worldly, loving and cruel, beautiful and harsh. The warriors who lived it have long since ridden up the Milky Way Trail to Se'han, the Place of the Dead. Walter Campbell used to say that he wanted to ride there with them.

FOREWORD

"THAT man," says Montaigne, "is truly unhappy who in his own house hath nowhere to be alone." Equally unfortunate is the man whose mind encloses no chosen region of the imagination into which he may at will retire from his usual pursuits.

Among the lords of such domains I count myself fortunate. I passed much time as a boy in Cheyenne camps, playing and swimming with the Indian boys, and winding my uncle's ponies in exciting races along the North Canadian. At that time much of the primitive Indian life remained. What I saw then is clear and vivid to this day, though I thought and understood as a child. But when I became a man, I could not bring myself to put away these childish things. Rather I read and studied and saw more of them, and so came to fill the pageant I had seen with the passion and meaning which a child cannot comprehend. This strange and fascinating Indian life, flashing against the calm background of eternal Nature, became my kingdom of imagination. There I roam and adventure as I please. I lie in wait to strike the enemy at dawn. I flay the smoking buffalo carcass. I feel the robe upon my naked shoulders and hear the sunscorched grass crunch beneath my moccasins. I hobble my ponies and pitch my tipi in happy hunting grounds. Hence my story and its title.

Yet this book is made of realities, not romance. Primitive man, never having learned to enjoy his emotions, had no sentimental feeling for the past, and his wildest stories were to him matter of fact. To the man who believes in fairies, they are as real and as concrete as a dog or a stone. The reader must expect no sentimental coloring, and such romantic qualities as the tale may have are inherent in the novelty of its setting. These Indians do not wear beaded moccasins and warbonnets on the hunt. Here is no dress parade, but a stark story of a rude and simple world, where men found happiness at grips with death.

The Arthurian legends were compiled by men far removed in time and spirit from the life represented, and I fancy that, in this respect at least, we are at no disadvantage in re-handling imaginatively the recorded legends and history of the Plains Indians. The great mass of material—myth, legend, history, stories of eye-witnesses, my own observations—upon which I have drawn, is an almost unworked mine. From this I have selected incidents not merely actual, but typical. However this venture may fare, I know that the materials available for such use are equal in power, in range, in variety, to those developed in the Sagas of the Norsemen.

My purpose is to present a comprehensive picture of Plains Indian life—the Indian seen against his proper background, as he was a century or more ago, without admixture of civilized conceptions. The difficulty in an attempt of this kind lies in the inability for the general reader—due to lack of opportunities for observation of Indians—to realize the physical aspect of aboriginal life. This difficulty, it is believed, has been overcome by the many excellent and accurate illustrations in the text.

In writing a book of this kind about a phase of life now long ended, I have been compelled to avail myself of the records of early observers, especially the books of Prince Maximilian von Wied, Catlin, the Journal of Alexander Henry the Younger, and the many volumes issued by the Bureau of American Ethnology, in the search for details of incident and description. My especial thanks are due to George Bent, Thunder Bull, Felix Roman Nose, Burnt All Over, Hubble Big Horse, and other Indian informants and interpreters for many of the stories, incidents, and details incorporated in this book. My friend John H. Seger, of Colony, Oklahoma, has given me much aid in understanding the old-time Indian. I am indebted for a number of suggestions and for most sympathetic co-operation to the illustrator, Mr. Frederick Weygold, my partner in this enterprise. His long intercourse with the Plains tribes has given him an understanding of them quite unparalleled, in my opinion, among American artists. His familiarity with Indian exhibits in museums abroad, where the earliest collections are to be found, has prepared him to illustrate early Indian life perhaps more accurately and truly than any other living American artist.

I wish also to mention the courtesy of the Field Museum, Chicago, where I was enabled to obtain exact copies of designs of painted tipis, weapons, clothing, furniture, etc., etc., which have been introduced into the illustrations and descriptions along with those from the collections of the illustrator.

STANLEY VESTAL

CONTENTS

ORIGINAL PAINTINGS
By Frederick Weygold

HAPPY HUNTING GROUNDS

The Calumet Dance

CHAPTER I

AFTER THE BATTLE

It was summer. The cottonwoods along the river shimmered in the hot noon sun. There was the silence of the prairie.

Suddenly an unkempt pinto loped wearily out of the shadow of the trees towards the ford. The lariat lashed round his lower jaw whipped his lathered shoulders and trailed beside him in the dust. At every jump his half-naked Indian rider struck the smoking flanks heavily with the quirt. The pony crossed the short stretch of sun-burnt grass, scuffled down the sandy bank and, spattering through the shallows, came to a stop and thrust its thirsty muzzle eye-deep into the muddy waters. The man knelt

3

on the pony's back to keep his moccasins dry, and showered blows mercilessly upon his heedless mount.

One after another, at the same desperate gait, other tired ponies emerged from the timber and splashed into the stream. They drank frantically for the brief moment allowed them by their masters. Then they scrambled out under the lash and stood with heaving sides, hanging their heads dejectedly in the noonday sun. The horsemen did not dismount. They slouched wearily, their naked legs dangling limply against the damp sides of their mounts. They said little, but watched anxiously the cottonwood grove from which they had just emerged.

At length another horseman came in sight. He was driving before him a pony on whose back lay a warrior. The man's thighs were lashed to the pony's barrel with a lariat, his hands were twisted in the pony's mane, his sagging head bobbed with every jump of the fagged animal. The pair splashed through the ford and out again, and came to a stop when the group was reached. Some of the warriors now dismounted, approached the wounded man, and gave him a drink. But they made no move to take him from the pony's back, badly hurt though he was. All the men displayed an anxiety to be gone that showed how desperate was their haste. Since gray dawn of the day before they had ridden almost without rest to escape the overwhelming numbers of their pursuing enemies, the Blackfeet, and every

4

hilltop showed the nearness of the cloud of dust which hung upon their rear and gained and gained. Their expedition had been a failure. They had been discovered and repulsed in the act of taking ponies from the Blackfoot camp. One had been killed there. It was doubtful whether the others could escape.

The wounded man struggled to raise his body to a sitting position on the pony's back, swept his dishevelled hair from before his bloodshot eyes, and spoke to his comrades.

"Friends, I can go no farther. My heart is poor. Take pity on me. Let me rest awhile."

Nothing was said to this, but it was apparent at once that the others would not entertain such a proposal. Behind came the Blackfeet, sure death to all who were overtaken. Ahead lay the safety of the palisaded Mandan village on the bluffs of the Missouri. It was their lives against him, and he saw they would not tarry. But the wounded man made no protest.

"Friends, I can go no farther. Leave me here on the trail where I can die fighting. Tell my comrades to avenge me."

No time was lost. Quickly the lariat about his thighs was loosened. They lowered him gently from the horse's back and laid him upon a buffalo robe spread in the shadow of a clump of young willows. They placed his lance and quiver beside him, gave him a handful of jerked beef—all the food they had—mounted without a word and rode rapidly away through the parched bottoms and over the hill.

Silence settled once more on the valley. Killer sat in the shadow of the willows facing the river. From his quiver of panther skin he took several arrows and thrust the points lightly into the ground before him, so that they would be handy. He satisfied himself that his bow was in order and laid it aside.

Whoever approached him must come in the open, and he counted upon killing several enemies before they reached him. Even then he would not be entirely helpless, for his lance was strong and well made, with a two-edged steel blade a foot long and as sharp as a razor. How soon his enemies might come he could not tell. He thought it would not be long.

The wounded man was well built, with the straight back, capacious chest, sinewy limbs, and small hands and feet of the typical Plains Indian. He carried his head proudly, and his face showed strength and poise. The nose was large and aquiline, the chin square and aggressive, the eyes steady, the mouth firm, with lips thrust out, as it were, in sinister curves. As he sat there nursing his roughly bandaged shin, few would have supposed that he had undergone such a ride with a broken leg and was now awaiting certain death.

It was very quiet. The breeze scarcely stirred the foliage of the willows. The midday sun beat down upon the dry, white sand about him with a dazzling glare, while the heat waves made the prairie beyond the river dance dizzily. Far up in the blue a buzzard circled on outstretched wings, watchful and alone. The afternoon sun sloped slowly towards the west, while Killer the Mandan scanned the sun-dazed terrain with fevered eyes.

Slowly the time dragged on, and the westering sun shifted the shadow of his shelter, so that he was obliged to move his position little by little to avoid its rays. Killer began to droop under the strain, though he sang his death-song over and over again. The song was a plaintive melody in a minor key, with many vocables and few words. It expressed briefly his bitter reproach to the Grizzly Bear, his guardian spirit, which had promised him—in a vision—safety in battle. The words of the song rose and fell on the vibrant melody with pathetic insistence:

"The Grizzly Bear has deceived me!"

Evening came, and the coyotes on the hill-tops round about yelped their chattering, shuddering protest at the mockery of life. When the sun went down the heat suddenly lifted, and the dry chill of night settled upon the plains. Killer drew his robe about him and shook with fever. It was clear to him that the Blackfeet had given up the case. He was left to die without a battle, to become the meat of crows and coyotes. His heart sank. Towards morning he became delirious and sang and shouted, rolling about upon the sand in imaginary battles with his foes, until at length he lay quiet in the cool earth among the roots of the willows. So he lay until his fever left him. His brain cleared and his empty stomach drove him to take stock of food. He ate sparingly of his handful of dried beef, crept painfully to the river for a drink, and slept again.

Next day his strength began to return, his spirits rose, and he was glad to find himself alive. His pony had deserted him and he made no attempt to travel, but lay quiet making plans and watching for a chance to knock down a rabbit or some larger animal on which to live until his leg would bear him. Occasionally he succeeded in adding a little fresh meat to his miserable fare. But his appetite was ravenous. So days passed. At last he found his leg apparently sound. He planned to start home that night.

The same afternoon a great dust swept over the hills a mile away. It rapidly advanced toward the river. As it came nearer, a thunder of hoofs shook the earth, and Killer could make out the sharp horns and swinging heads of fleeing buffalo. Flanking the herd and thrust boldly into the midst of it, half hidden by the swirling dust, trained buffalo ponies carried their naked riders in hot pursuit of the fat cows, while in the rear the heavier, less speedy bulls labored frantically to maintain the pace. Straight towards the river they came, where Killer watched in dismay, unable as he was to run out of the path of the trampling hoofs. But the leaders swerved at the river bank and swept away into the timber, leaving the bottom land studded with the black carcasses of dead and dying buffalo.

When the dust cleared away, Killer could see the hunters, singly and in groups, running down wounded animals. One of these, her sides bristling with feathered shafts, plunged through the stream and stopped a short distance from the wounded man. The cow faced her pursuers doggedly, turning with surprising agility as they maneuvered, propping herself upon her failing limbs and shaking her head threateningly as it drooped lower and lower between her forelegs, heaving and groaning, while blood and slaver poured from her muzzle upon the trampled grass. The hunters rode round and round the dying cow, jerking arrow after arrow from their quivers and sending them into the vitals of their game. At last the animal seemed to become unconscious of their presence. The eyes glazed, the legs stiffened, and the great carcass toppled of a sudden to the ground.

Scarcely had it done so when the hunters dismounted, tied their ponies to the creature's horns, drew out their arrows, and were at work skinning and cutting up the carcass. So expert were they that in a few minutes the hide had been removed and the animal reduced to a heap of quivering ruins. Not a stroke of the knife was wasted or went astray. The flesh from the ribs was sliced away, the vitals removed and cleaned, the limbs severed and divided, the ribs broken from the backbone by blows from one of the animal's legs used as a hammer, and the whole securely packed in the hide upon the backs of pack horses brought up by boys from the rear.

Killer stared hungrily from his hiding place at the juicy, dark red meat. And when the hunters paused in their butchering to enjoy the tidbit of warm, raw liver seasoned with gall, the starving man licked his lips and swallowed, and only strong self-control prevented him from leaving his refuge and hobbling to the feast.

He knew the hunters were Cheyennes, a tribe with which his people had no quarrel. But he knew the customs of the plains too well to trust himself to the mercy of strangers in the open. A scalp is a scalp. He himself would not have scrupled to kill a lone Cheyenne under like circumstances. So he took no chances.

Soon the prairie became alive with Indians—hunters returning jauntily on their buffalo ponies, boys and women with strings of pack animals and travois coming out to dress and carry home the meat. Starving though he was, Killer forgot his hunger in his anxiety to escape detection. He lay motionless, alert to every movement on the prairie. No one found him. Even the lean dogs which came prowling and sniffing to find a little blood where a carcass had been cut up were too intent upon their search to trouble him. An Indian butcher leaves no offal, and the smell of the kill only intensified the ravenous appetites of the dogs and made them indifferent to everything else.

All afternoon until night the pack trains, one after another, passed Killer's hiding place loaded with good things and vanished over the hill on their way to the Cheyenne camp, leaving the scene of the hunt as barren of food as he had found it. But Killer was not reassured. Alone, disabled, starving, and afoot, his chances of escape from a region hourly patrolled by the young men of the Cheyenne camp were poor indeed. To remain where he was meant starvation. To start for home meant a long and painful journey in momentary danger of death. But if he could reach the Cheyenne camp undetected, he might be able to steal a good pony and be miles away before the Cheyennes discovered their loss. In any case he might get meat from a drying-scaffold. And once inside their camp he might count on protection from the same men who would have killed him as a matter of course on the open prairie.

When it was night and the prairie had long been empty of life, Killer made a tiny fire well screened from view, and smoothed the sand before him with his hand. On the smooth place he laid a glowing coal from the fire. He took from the small pouch fastened to his belt a handful of cedar leaves and poured them upon the hot coal. As the white smoke rose through the still air, he bathed his hands in its incense and rubbed them upon his body, his limbs, and his head. This rite of purification ended, he took from the pouch a small pipe such as warriors carry—short and thick, fashioned from the leg bone of a deer and bound tightly against the heat with heavy strands of sinew knotted and shrunk about it. The larger end of this straight tube he filled with the last remnants of his tobacco, and holding it upright before him, addressed the Mysterious Powers which held his life in their keeping.

"Master of Life, behold this pipe. Smoke it. I do not ask to kill anybody. I only want to take food and get horses. I ask you to help me. I will now smoke this pipe in your honor. I have let my breasts be pierced in the Medicine Lodge. I have shed much blood. I ask you to protect me and give me long life. Let me take good horses!"

Killer lighted the pipe, smoked it, and put it away. He smothered the ashes of his fire and got stiffly to his feet. He threw his quiver about his shoulders, and dragging his robe by one corner and supporting himself with his lance, he slowly and painfully crossed the stream and followed the trail of the buffalo hunters.

Laboriously he crossed the bottoms and mounted the slope. Beyond this lay several gentle swells of the prairie, and he limped across these as well, his trained eye following without difficulty the converging trails of the pack trains. His progress was very slow. Often he stopped to rest. But at last he paused on the top of the last rise. At his feet ran a shallow, wooded stream and beyond this, white

and ghostly in the moonlight, rose the great circle
of the Cheyenne camp.

CHAPTER II

THE CHEYENNE INDIAN CAMP

KILLER lay among the bunchgrass on the hilltop east of the Cheyenne camp. To the south the dark timber and high, barren bluffs beyond stretched dimly away on his left, marking the course of the river from which he had just come. Beyond the camp a high ridge cut off all view to the west. On his right, to the north of the camp, a small stream issued lazily from among scattered groups of trees, and hugging the line of tipis on that side, passed beneath the little bluff on which he lay, then angled away towards the river. Across this stream and just below him, on a level, grassy flat, stood the camp.

The tipis were pitched at intervals with considerable regularity, the whole camp forming a great horseshoe with the opening or entrance to the north. Close within this circle of white tipis appeared a dark ring of picketed ponies. The large central space was unoccupied save by dark masses which Killer knew to be herds of less valuable horses.

The scattered trees along the little creek mingled with the tipis on that side of the circle, so that it was impossible to make an accurate count of them from where Killer lay. On the farther side the tents melted into a vague white blur in the moonlight. Nevertheless, he counted more than a hundred tipis, not including the many small shelters used as kitchens or sunshades during the day. Two hundred warriors and more were in that camp—with plenty of ponies, he reflected. If he succeeded in getting away on one of their mounts he would be lucky, considering his weakened condition.

Killer had been a long time reaching the camp, and the night was far gone. But he knew that after a successful hunt there would be much feasting and merrymaking. Many of the people would be awake and abroad all night. Fresh meat was not to be had every day. He waited a long time, watching the camp.

Everywhere among the lodges small outdoor cooking fires leaped and danced where people were still picking over the huge piles of meat and roasting their favorite portions on sticks before the blaze. Here and there a tipi glowed yellow through the

night as the firelight played against its covering of
hides above the shoulders of the gamblers and
talkers within. He could hear the dull thudding of
a drum, and when the breeze served, a wisp of song
or the shrill, quavering yelp of a dancer. Dark forms
flitted about the fires, weird and unearthly against
the pale, drifting smoke. From the trees beyond the
camp came the full, clear notes of a flute, monoto-
nously repeating a lover's call to his chosen maiden
in a nearby tipi. Groups of serenaders moved
around the circle in their white robes, stopping to
partake of the hospitality of the feasters about the
fires. At intervals, Killer could hear the wild, wailing cries of some family of mourners, rising and
dying away like the melancholy voice of a wolf.
Gradually the fires died down, the sounds of merriment became less frequent. Still Killer lay on the
hilltop. Above him the solemn constellations, showing blue and faint in the moonlight, wheeled slowly
across the sky. Once a dog raised a long, dismal
howl which was taken up by others and still others
around the circle until all the dogs of the camp
added their baying and yelping to the hideous
chorus, producing a weird and discordant clamor
at once fierce and mournful, which died away as
suddenly as it began. Slowly the moon dropped
towards the west. Killer waited until all sound and
movement had ceased and the great camp seemed
to sleep.

He thought best to approach the camp from the
north, where the tipis near the entrance almost

touched the trees along the creek. Warily he drew
near the little stream, took off his moccasins, waded
it noiselessly, and crept into the gloom beneath the
trees, moving as silently as a shadow.

At a little distance the tipis stood stiff and trim
in the moonlight. They were all new, of buffalo hide
whitened with clay, each one bearing on high its
lofty crown of poles. Beside each one stood the
small kitchen-shelter—an old tipi cut down—sprawl-
ing on its poles high above the ground like a gigantic daddy-long-legs. Nearby the travois were
stacked together in a pyramid to keep their rawhide
lashings from hungry teeth of prowling dogs and
wolves. Here and there a fresh hide was pegged to
the ground or streched upon an upright frame in
process of dressing. Tethered ponies cropped the
grass, close to the tipis of their owners. The space
between the lodges was filled by a series of scaffolds

made of peeled poles and rawhide cords stretched back and forth, on which heavy curtains of thinly sliced buffalo flesh had been hung to dry in the sun. So much meat had been killed that the whole camp seemed to be fenced in by thin sheets of flesh. The sight of all this good living was tempting to the hungry man, and when the breeze favored, his nostrils delighted in the odor of fresh meat, which blended pleasantly with the familiar camp scents of home—horsemint, woodsmoke, rawhide, and horses.

He crept silently through the timber until he stood in the shadow of the last tree. Beyond this there was no shelter between him and the nearest tipi. The moon was still high enough to flood the open with light and to smother the trees in blackest shadow. He paused to listen. All was silent save the ceaseless, impersonal insect voice of the night and the soft snuffle of a grazing pony blowing the dust from its nostrils. Killer looked carefully about him. No one stirred, though a few dying fires still winked and flickered fitfully about the circle. Now was the time. He had come to the end of the line of tents.

There a great painted tipi stood proudly on guard over the entrance to the camp. Killer knew that the position of that tipi marked its owner as a man of courage and prominence in the tribe. The size and beauty of the dwelling bore out this belief. It was adorned and painted in a lavish fashion, and dominated all the lodges near it. High above the smoke-hole from the tip of the tallest pole a long, thick horsetail swung in the night breeze to mark the home of a chief. A buffalo's head was painted on the door.

Near the door were picketed two horses, and on these the eyes of Killer rested with admiration. One was a magnificent black stallion with white face and stockings, showing the slender legs, the long body, the size, bone, and general development of the carefully bred Spanish horse of northern Mexico, proud of his Arab ancestry. The other was a typical product of the indiscriminate coupling and winter hardships of the prairie horses—small, tough, deer-legged, big-barreled, with slanting quarters, mulish hocks, a hide fantastically flared and blotched with white, and one wicked glass eye that showed the latent devil in his heart.

These were the war horses of the chief—animals whose backs never carried any load other than the body of their master. Such horses were not to be seen among the tribes to the north. For such an animal Killer had known a man to give one of his wives, three horses, and the value of fifty beaver.

Like all Plains Indians, Killer loved the horse. Without it, his ancestors had been starving skulkers in the woods, following the deer on foot, laboriously digging pits to entrap antelope, or grubbing with a hoe about the roots of corn and bean plants. With the horse, stolen from his enemies or caught running wild on the plains, the Indian became master of a boundless domain, certain of his food—the buffalo—able to make sudden war against his enemies, rich, proud, arrogant, insolent, master of a freedom before undreamed. For the horse of the plains, though never groomed, living on grass in summer and the bark of cottonwoods in winter, had no superior as a saddle animal. It had as much sense as a mule, as much hardihood and endurance as a prairie wolf, and a "hard stomach" that enabled it to stand any amount of hard riding and to go without proper food and water for unbelievable periods. Killer burned with desire as he watched the two, noting every point appreciatively, with all the interest and enthusiasm of the life-long horseman. He would cut their lariats and ride away home, he thought. He would ride the black and lead the pinto. He pictured himself dashing in among the earth lodges of the Mandan village, singing his song of triumph, the only one of all his war party who had anything to show for the foray against the Blackfeet. With such a horse under him, the Cheyennes could never overtake him. But first he must have food.

Killer wrapped his buffalo robe about him and limped boldly out into the moonlight. The robe concealed his face and head, and he felt sure that he would not be recognized at a little distance as a stranger. A few steps brought him behind the painted tipi, where he began to strip a scaffold of its meat. Greedily he gobbled down bits of fat and raw flesh. A great sheet of back-tallow hung there, and from this he pulled large pieces and thrust them into his mouth. A long blood sausage writhed among the slabs of meat, festooned from pole to pole. Killer seized it, cut it open, and sucked the fluid contents. He was about to snatch off a few tongues that hung there, on which to live while riding home. But at that moment a dog in the second tipi barked sharply. At once a dozen others took up the cry. Killer stepped quickly behind the upright frame on which a fresh hide was stretched and prepared to defend himself, still noiselessly munching his mouthful of raw meat. But the dog suddenly relapsed into silence with an agonized yelp and a whimper, as some one in the lodge struck it with a stick of firewood. The other dogs grew quiet. The only sound was the steady *crop crop* of a grazing pony.

Killer hobbled quickly to the horses. The pinto was wary and alert, threw up its head, and trotted in a half circle at the limit of its tether, evading his clumsy advances. The black, a proud animal, retreated to the end of its lariat, swung round as the rope brought it up short, and threw up its head. There it stood with nervous, rigid ears, blowing softly with surprise at the stranger. Killer approached it, following the lariat hand over hand, and managed to place his hand upon the animal's trembling back. Quickly he looped the lariat about its lower jaw and attempted to swing himself up. But the restive black moved away whenever Killer approached its side, and the man's game leg prevented his leaping upon the horse's back, as he would have done otherwise. The more anxiously he struggled,

the more nervous the horse became, until at length
it broke away from him and snorted with dislike.

Again the dog barked from the tipi. There was a
sound of voices. The movements of the horses had
been heard. Some one came out of the second tipi
and Killer could hear the crisp sound of moccasins
crunching the sun-parched buffalo grass. A moment
later the figure of a man moved in dark silhouette
against the whiteness of the neighboring tipi. Killer
dropped the lariat and drew his robe about him.
He could not get away with the animal now. To
advance into the camp he must face this man. To go
in the other direction would cause suspicion, prob-

ably discovery. He was no condition to kill and make his escape on foot.

At once Killer made his decision. He stooped and fastened the lariat to the peg at his feet. Before the man reached the painted tipi, Killer deliberately turned, walked to the door, mumbling something indistinguishable. He lifted the flap, placed his foot inside, stooped, and entered. In like manner a rattle-snake slips quietly into the open door of the prairie-dog's hole to make himself at home there until he may devour the young of his host.

Inside all was dim and indistinct, for the fire was very low. The tipi was a large one—some twenty feet in diameter—and Killer could make out the sleeping figures of the family on the low couches about the fire. He paused for a moment on the threshold, but no one stirred. He heard the steps of the inquisitive man outside returning to his own tipi, and his low voice as he explained to those within that everything was all right. Then Killer advanced, threw off his robe, and sat down by the fire, his back to the door. He kept the point of his lance towards the back of the tipi, the place where the owner should be sleeping. As his eyes grew accustomed to the gloom, he could make out two figures on the couch at the back. To his right lay a boy, half covered by his robe. Opposite slept the mother of the chief, an old woman whose eyes knew no more light by day than by night. The tipi was richly furnished. The beds were all made of mats of peeled willow rods, painted and adorned with tassels and quill-work. Painted rawhide bags and cases hung from the lodge poles and at the heads of the beds, and the weapons of the chief and his son hung within easy reach above their heads. Killer had chosen well, he thought. If *this* man received him, the others would not dare attack him.

There was meat stew in the kettle simmering on the embers. So Killer, having had enough of raw food, took the big spoon of ram's-horn that lay there, and helped himself. As he ate he felt his strength and confidence returning, for the warm stew was very good.

Whirlwind, the Cheyenne chief, slept on his couch at the back of the lodge in the place of honor. But A-nu'tah, the wife of Whirlwind, was not yet asleep. She had seen Killer come into the tipi, and she could not tell who he was. She touched her husband, and waked him, and whispered—

"Who is this man beside the fire? Get up and see what he wants."

But Whirlwind was unconcerned. It was the custom for a hungry man to enter any tipi and eat, if food was ready. Whirlwind was a great chief and he was ashamed to say to a man, "Who are you, and what are you doing in my lodge?" So he said to his wife—

"Let him eat. Perhaps he is hungry."

There were many visitors in the camp. Whirlwind turned to his sleep again. But the woman could not tell who the man was, for the fire was very low. So she lay quiet and watched him.

The chief's pipe and tobacco pouch lay beside the fire. And when Killer had eaten enough, he took tobacco from the bag and filled the pipe and lighted it. He had had no good tobacco for a long time, and this was very good. He offered smoke to the Mysterious Powers because his life had been spared.

A-nu'tah was still awake. She roused her husband and said—

"Look! Who is this man who smokes your pipe in the lodge? Get up and see what he wants, for his hunger is satisfied."

Then Whirlwind was angry, and said—

"Woman, go to sleep! Let him smoke! Perhaps he has no tobacco."

Whirlwind was ashamed because of the words of his wife. For he was a great chief, and his tipi was open to all comers. So he would not get up, and turned to sleep again.

When the pipe was smoked out, Killer wrapped himself in his robe, and lay by the fire and slept there. But A-nu'tah, the wife of Whirlwind, watched him all this while.

CHAPTER III

THE BOY HUNTER

EARLY next morning, before it was light, Ki'as, the son of Whirlwind, took his lariat and quiver and left the tipi to drive in his father's ponies. The boy was ambitious to become a warrior, and it was a point of pride with him to be first up in the lodge. At dawn his first thought was always of his pony. For he did everything he saw the warriors do.

The morning star blazed white in the east when the boy reached the prairie where the ponies had been turned loose the night before. They were not there, so Ki'as turned towards the river. He knew that when the horses had eaten their fill they must have gone to the river for a drink. He followed an old trail, worn deep in the red clay of the prairie by the hoofs of hundreds of buffalo going to drink, and washed still deeper by the pouring rains of many years. In places, where the trail descended a steep bank, the boy's head scarcely cleared the edge of the cut, so deep it was.

When he reached the river it was growing light. There were many head in the grassy bottoms, but after a while Ki'as found his pony. He approached and, as the pony started off, threw one end of the lariat across its back. At once the animal stopped dead and stood without moving a muscle while Ki'as tied the rope to its lower jaw and jumped on its back. The pony knew from hard experience what happened if a horse tried to break away when the noose fell upon its shoulders, and the mere touch of a rope was enough to stop it in its tracks.

Ki'as began to round up his father's horses to drive them back to camp. He galloped back and forth through the bottoms, swinging the free end of his lariat about his head and shouting, heading back the runaways. Whirlwind had a great many horses, of every condition, shape, and size, white, black, red, gray, mottled and splashed with a motley variety of colors. They all had a wild and startled look and nimbly avoided the knotted end of the boy's hair rope. They evidently regarded their human masters much as they did the big gray timber wolves which harassed them in winter and kept them standing in a circle, heads together and flying heels out, through the long bitter nights. Soon

Ki'as had them well bunched and headed back towards the camp, their backs rising and falling as they ran like the waves of the sea.

But one horse broke from the herd and ran into the brush in the bend of the river. Ki'as knew the animal of old. It was as ugly as it was tough and wary—a Roman-nosed, slit-eared, cow-hocked, stump-sucking brute. Its head and ewe neck joined like the two parts of a hammer. Its shag, mouse-colored coat and thin tail were filled with burs. Its mane fell to right and left indifferently in half a dozen places. The poor beast's barrel was a veritable hogshead, distended as it was by the bushels of green grass it had gorged, and its back and high withers showed raw and sore where the sharp corners of a vicious pack saddle had lacerated them. But the pony's crowning beauty was an enormous blue-black mustache which sprouted symmetrically on the upper lip below either nostril and spiraled luxuriantly outwards to twin points. The Cheyennes called the horse Bull Tail, after a whiskered chief of the Kiowa Indians. The animal deserved the name, for it was as tricky as any Kiowa, and as clever at making trouble. The women always tied its forefeet together with a rawhide strap before turning it loose. But the horse had learned to use its forefeet together in a lumbering, jumping gallop that covered the ground surprisingly fast, so that the strap made no difference. Hobbled as Bull Tail was, Ki'as had to ride his hardest to head the refractory beast back to camp.

As the boy rode through the willows and tall weeds and rushes in the wake of Bull Tail, quirting his pony, suddenly a yellow buffalo calf started up before him and ran away through the brush with its short tail stuck up in the air, bawling for its mother. The calf was alone, having been separated from the herd when the Cheyennes made their hunt the day before.

When Ki'as saw the calf he thought no more about the horses. He had never hunted buffalo. He was only a boy. His arrows were blunt, with wooden heads such as boys use to kill birds and rabbits. But he had one war arrow which he had taken from his father's quiver. It was as long as his arm, straight, smooth, well notched, winged with three trimmed turkey feathers glued down and lashed on with sinew. The shaft had three shallow, wavering grooves along its length to make it fly straight, and carried a long triangular head of sharp iron. Below the notch was painted the mark of his father. The possession of this arrow made the boy feel more like a warrior. So he had kept it in his quiver.

Ki'as took this arrow from his quiver, fitted it to his bow, and rode hard after the frightened calf, drubbing the pony's sides with his heels. He tried to get alongside where he would have a chance to kill, for he had heard the hunters tell how a buffalo must be killed. He knew that he must pierce the chafed spot behind the crook of the foreleg if he wished to strike the vital place. He had only one

arrow and he did not intend to waste it. But the scared calf ran hard, dodging and turning through the thick brush so that it was difficult to follow, much less gain position for the shot. A buffalo calf looks a clumsy, shapeless creature, with its block head, its stumpy tail, its coat of the color and texture of a Teddy-bear. But it is surprisingly agile and usually keeps abreast of its mother when the buffalo run.

However, this calf had had nothing to eat since the day before, and soon it began to tire. It turned out of the brush into the open, and Ki'as saw his chance. He rode alongside the lumbering creature, took careful aim, put all his strength into the pull, and let fly the arrow. It went true, and deep into the side of the little buffalo. At once the calf stopped and stood with heaving sides and protruding tongue, moaning pitifully. Its head drooped lower and lower between the forelegs until it suddenly sank to the ground.

Ki'as was very proud of his first buffalo. By the time the calf was dead, many of the young men had come down after their ponies and stopped to inspect the kill. As for the horses, the boy had forgotten all about them.

When it was light, Whirlwind awoke and saw the stranger sitting by the fire. He knew him for a Mandan by the manner in which his hair was dressed, for it was parted from ear to ear. The back hair hung in many tails down the back, and the front hair was divided into three thick locks cut short, hanging about the face. The Cheyennes ranged and raided from the Saskatchewan River for into Mexico, and from the Missouri to the Great Shining Mountains. They knew the people of the plains. Whirlwind told his women to prepare food for the Mandan, and filled his long-stemmed pipe. There was no quarrel between the Cheyennes and the Mandans.

A-nu'tah brought dried buffalo meat in a wooden bowl, and Killer ate what was placed before him. Then Whirlwind lighted his pipe and passed it to his guest and the two men smoked together. When the pipe was smoked out, Whirlwind questioned his visitor.

Many small tribes ranged over the great plains following the buffalo, each one speaking its own tongue, which was usually quite unintelligible to the others. Yet the people of these many languages constanly met in hunting, in war, in trade, and in religious ceremonies, and found some ready means of communication absolutely necessary. In response to this need there grew up a wonderfully comprehensive and graphic speech or language of signs in which all Plains Indians could converse with ease and speed. So expressive and complete this language became that it could express every idea with which the Indian mind was familiar and with such fluency and ease and speed that it was in everyday use even among persons of the same camp and tribe. The Cheyennes were particularly expert in this gesture speech, owing to their constant intercourse with the Arapahos, their close allies, whose spoken language was utterly different from their own. In the sign language, then, Whirlwind questioned Killer. For the spoken language of the Cheyennes was as different from that of the Mandans as Greek is from German.

Then Killer told his story with quick, expressive gestures and graphic mimicry—how he had ridden two days to escape the pursuing Blackfeet, wounded as he was, until he could go no farther; how he had waited beside the trail for the enemy that never came; how he had been like to die, and how he had recovered; how he had followed the hunters to camp to find food and protection in the tipis of his brothers the Cheyennes. But he said nothing of his attempt to steal the war horse of his host.

Whirlwind saw that his guest was a brave man. He embraced Killer and said, "Friend, my heart is glad because you are here. Stay in my tipi until you are strong and able to travel."

Then Killer said, "Good! I will stay." So it was settled.

After a while, when the young men came driving in their ponies from the river, one of them rode to the tipi of Whirlwind and called out to him, "Ki'as has killed a buffalo calf in the bend of the river."

When the chief heard that, he cried out, "*A hó, a hó!* (Thanks, thanks!)" and jumping up, took a gun from above his bed and ran out of the tipi. He fired the gun in the air and gave it to an old man named Seven Bulls, who happened to be passing the tipi. To Seven Bulls he said, "Cry the camp. My son has killed a buffalo!"

Then the old man walked towards the center of the great circle of tipis singing a song of thanks for the gift of the gun. When he reached the middle of the circle, he called out in a loud, high-pitched, carrying voice, facing every part of the camp in turn, and repeating his words, "Ki'as, the son of Whirlwind, has killed a buffalo!" Everyone in the camp and many on the prairie beyond heard him, for Seven Bulls was a good crier. He had a good voice, and he was witty, so that people listened to what he said, for fear they might miss something good. So the whole camp knew that Ki'as had killed his first buffalo.

But Whirlwind jumped on his black war horse and rode without saddle or bridle towards the bend of the river to see the calf his son had killed. For the boy was the pride of his life, and he hoped that Ki'as would prove a great man.

Meanwhile one of his wives took the travois from behind the tipi and laid it upon the shoulders of a sore-backed pack horse. She climbed up and got astraddle of the animal and started him off with her quirt, riding after the chief to bring in the meat that Ki'as had killed. A-nu'tah remained in the tipi. She was the favorite wife of Whirlwind and managed it so that the other women did the heavy work. The mother of Ki'as was dead.

In the tipi the old mother of Whirlwind sat pounding dried beef into powder with a stone hammer, preparatory to making pemmican of it. She was blind, but she knew her work, and none of the meat was lost. Near her A-nu'tah was busy with deft fingers, laying colored porcupine quills upon a moccasin for her husband. She was a handsome woman, still young and graceful, with an oval face, fine white teeth, and luxuriant black hair. Her small, daintily shod feet showed beneath the scalloped skirt of her leather smock at one side. The smock itself was well cut and fell about her in heavy folds of soft brown buckskin having all the beautifully varied color and texture of Indian tanned leather, and adorned with long fringes and quillwork of beautiful design and pleasing colors. Her temples were touched with vermilion. As her rounded forearms moved through the soft fringes of her sleeves, now concealed and again revealing all their silver bracelets, Killer thought he had never seen a woman so attractive. He looked at her as a man looks at a pretty woman. His glances pleased

A-nu'tah, for he was a stranger and well built, and she thought him a brave man. So they sat, watching one another. And after a time they talked together in the silent language of signs. No one knew of this. For the mother of Whirlwind was blind.

The chief found his son beside the calf he had killed, and listened proudly while the boy told the story of his hunt. It was no mean feat to kill the first buffalo at a gallop with one arrow. Whirlwind felt sure that his son would be a great man. Two old men were wading in the shallows, spearing fish in the holes under the river bank. Whirlwind called to them to come and see the buffalo which Ki'as had killed. So the two old men came out of the water, their brown shanks glistening wet in the sunlight, to inspect the animal and hear the boy's story. They praised him and told him he would be a great warrior and feast-maker, and offered their services in cutting up the carcass. For the men who butcher the buffalo receive certain portions for their services, and the old men saw that the calf was in prime condition.

Whirlwind and his son rode back to camp, driving in the ponies, Bull Tail among the rest. They said little, but they were very happy.

After the chief reached his tipi, he dismounted and sat down on his couch at the back of the lodge and spoke to his wife. At once the women cleared the lodge of household goods and strewed grass all around the walls. On the grass they spread buffalo and bear skins to make comfortable seats, and built a small fire in the center. In the kitchen outside the tipi they made a fire under a brass kettle and cooked food.

Whirlwind put on his robe and stood in the door of his tipi. He called out the names of the principal men in the camp, one after another, repeating each one several times, asking the men to "come to his lodge, eat, and smoke." He wished to make a feast in honor of his son who that day had killed his first buffalo. Then Whirlwind took his seat on the couch in the place of honor opposite the tipi door. Ki'as sat beside his father. And Killer the Mandan took his seat in the lodge also.

After a time the guests began to gather, each one bringing his wooden bowl to eat from. They came in and found seats on the robes around the lodge. The women brought food in brass kettles and passed it through the door of the tipi. Two young men sitting near the door got up and carried the kettles around the lodge, serving the guests with spoons of yellow ram's-horn. Every man helped himself. But Whirlwind and Ki'as did not eat, because the feast was in their tipi. Indian hosts did not eat with their guests.

While the guests were eating, the chief mixed tobacco with the bark of the red willow and filled his pipe, tamping the mixture into the red stone bowl with a long carven tamper. When all had finished, he took a coal from the fire with a bent twig, lighted the pipe, and passed it to his neighbor. All the guests smoked, passing the pipe from hand to hand, inhaling deeply and blowing the smoke in long streams from their nostrils. While the pipe was circulating, Whirlwind told the story of his son's exploit. The men all applauded and praised the boy, prophesying great things of him in the future.

Then Gray Thunder stood up, drawing his robe about his hips. He was a famous warrior, one of the chiefs of the Dog Soldiers, though he wore only two eagle feathers in his hair. His war record was known to all. He began to tell one of his exploits against the Pawnees, speaking forcefully in a low tone, with many graphic gestures. His eyes gleamed, and the bear's-claw necklace upon his naked chest rose and fell with the excitement of his narrative. His hearers seemed to see the fight in all its details. When he reached the climax of his story—where he struck the enemy—all present beat upon the ground with stick or their bare hands, crying aloud and applauding with enthusiasm, "*Ho! ho!*"

Having thus demonstrated his fitness to perform the ceremony, Gray Thunder formally "threw away" the boyhood name Ki'as. The lad's exploit, he said, made him worthy of a new name, a warrior's name. Gray Thunder chose that of the boy's uncle, a distinguished warrior of the Eaters Band.

"My son," he said, "hereafter your name is Little Chief."

Then Whirlwind thanked his guest Gray Thunder, and gave him a good horse because of the compliment he had done the chief in changing his son's name.

Immediately after, the relatives of the boy brought presents to him, one a pony, another a man's quiver full of arrows, another a decorated robe, and so on. The family was proud of the boy who had killed the buffalo. All the camp knew of this. For the sides of the tipi were raised on account of the heat, and the people crowded about the tipi to hear what was said.

Now the Cheyennes were curious to know who the Mandan was and how he came to be sitting in the lodge of their chief. So Whirlwind asked Killer to tell his story to the men in the tipi.

Killer, using the vivid language of signs, quickly told his story as he had told it to the chief. This was his story: "We went on the warpath against the

Blackfeet. We had traveled seven days when the scouts came back and said, 'The Crow Indians are hunting buffalo ahead of us over that ridge.' We went on and saw two Crow Indians. One had a gun, the other a bow and arrows. They pointed their weapons at us, but we rode up and killed them both. We saw more Crows a long way off running buffalo, but they did not see us. We went on to the country of the Blackfeet. The edge of the river was heavily timbered, and beyond the river was the Blackfoot camp. We hid in the timber until nearly morning. Then we put on our war paint and went into the village and took many ponies. The others wanted to go home. But I was not satisfied. I wanted hair. So I ran back to the camp and entered a lodge which had a yellow buffalo painted over the door. When I entered, a dog sprang up and barked. It was so dark inside the lodge I could see nothing. Someone cried out and fired a gun at me. The lodge was full of smoke and my ears rang with the noise of the gun. But I was not hit. I jumped towards the place where the gun had flashed, stabbing with my knife, but the Blackfoot had rolled out of the tent under the side. Outside I could hear the Blackfeet running out of their lodges, yelling and shooting. I ran out of the lodge, looking for our horses. I could hear the Blackfeet behind me, running and shooting at me. They kept firing at me and I dodged back and forth, running all the time, trying not to be hit. One of my young men saw me coming. He was in a sheltered place and called out to me, 'Come on over here!' He was on horseback. I ran to him. We sat double on his horse. But just as we started off, a bullet hit me and broke one of the bones of my leg— here, below the knee! We rode hard and caught up with the others. When we reached the horses, I was helped on to one of my own, tied on with a lariat. One of my young men was killed, and we lost all the horses we had taken except the ones we rode. We rode as fast as we could all that day and night and the next day until noon. I could go no farther. I told my comrades to leave me by the trail and I would die fighting. But the Blackfeet never came."

This was the story Killer told the Cheyennes. But he did not tell them why he had gone on the war-path against the Blackfeet, for that would have made him a laughing-stock.

It happened in this way:

The Mandans had left their palisaded village of earth lodges on the bluffs of the Missouri and had gone after buffalo, living in tipis like those of the Cheyennes. After they had killed all the meat they could use, the men had feasted and gambled and made merry while the women dressed the hides and dried the meat. They made so much noise drumming and yelling that all the game was frightened away from the neighborhood. For the excitement of the gambling ran very high, and large stakes were won and lost. Killer was a rich man among the Mandans. He had a white buffalo robe, and many ponies, three wives, and two guns, and everything that a man of his people could desire.

When the gambling began, he gambled with the others. But the luck was against him. First he lost his ponies, then his robes, his tipi, his guns, and his clothing. But he would not quit loser. He put his wives "on the blanket" and lost them too. And when he had nothing left but the breechcloth and moccasins he stood in, he walked through the camp, wailing aloud and calling on his relatives, "Take pity on me!"

After a time his relatives took pity on him and brought presents—one a lodge, another a pony, a third a robe, another a weapon, and so no, until Killer could shelter himself again. But he could not buy a wife to care for his tipi because he had no ponies to give, and no one wished to marry his daughter to a man who put his wives "on the blanket" when he gambled. The men who had won his wives were not his relatives and they would not give back the women.

As Killer went about the camp gathering his gifts together, he came to the lodge of his nephew. His nephew gave him a bed complete, with mattress and mats of peeled willow rods to hang at the head and foot, painted and decorated, and fancy buckskin pillows stuffed with buffalo wool. It was very handsome, such as a bride makes for her marriage-bed.

When Killer came out of his nephew's tipi carrying the bed, an old wrinkled hag sitting under a kitchen shelter nearby saw him. She laughed and cackled, shrieking at him so that all the camp could hear, "Where is the wife to go with the marriage-bed?" Then all the people joined in the laugh at Killer. He was ashamed. For he could not get a woman to care for his lodge.

When the chiefs heard what had happened, they agreed that Killer must have a wife. But they thought he needed a lesson. They were unwilling to give him back all his women. The wives of Killer were of different ages. One was young and handsome, another fat and cheerful, and the third a weazened old hag, broken and scarred by years of heavy work and rough weather, who looked old enough to be her husband's mother. The chiefs sent presents to the man who had won this old woman and told him to send her back to Killer, so that Killer would have some one to care for his tipi. The old woman came back. And again the whole camp made merry over Killer, because he had got back the ugly old wife he liked least of all.

Then he told his wife to make many moccasins and pack them well with pemmican, because he was going on the warpath. He could not endure the laughter of his people, and burned to do something brave that would turn their ridicule into respect. When the moccasins were ready and filled with meat, he took his lariat and his weapons and started by night on the warpath to take horses and scalps from the Blackfeet. When he was well outside the camp, certain young men who had seen the preparations in his tipi overtook him and said they would go along.

Every night the dreams of Killer were bad. He dreamed he saw one of his young men lying scalped near a Blackfoot camp. He knew that this was a bad sign. But he was ashamed to return empty-handed to his people. He was afraid to go on. But his shame was greater than his fear. So he said nothing about his bad dreams to the young men, but went on as though he had had no warning. This was the origin of Killer's expedition against the Blackfeet. But of all this he said nothing to the Cheyennes gathered in the tipi. He knew that, if he did, they would despise him.

When Killer had finished his story, the Cheyennes applauded. They saw that he was a brave man. He was invited to eat in many tipis. For the Cheyennes loved bravery above all things.

Then an old chief said, "Now is a good time, while we are all together, to talk of the coming of the Sioux." The others approved his suggestion. So the feast became a council, and the men talked of their plans for the Calumet Dance which the Sioux were coming to make with the Cheyennes. And when the council was over, Whirlwind cleaned the ashes from his pipe and tapped the pipe bowl with the tamper and said, "It is finished." The guests took their food bowls and left the tipi, singing songs of praise in honor of their chief and his son, who that day had killed his first buffalo.

When the Mandan learned that the Sioux were expected in the Cheyenne camp, he was disturbed. The Sioux and the Mandans were enemies, and he could not tell what might happen. He questioned his host, using the language of signs. But Whirlwind said, "Friend, fear nothing. You have eaten in my tipi." But nevertheless he saw the Mandan was still troubled.

Then Whirlwind led his guest out of the tipi. The chief took the lariat of the pinto picketed beside the lodge and placed the hand of the Mandan about it, close up to the animal's neck. The lariat was of plaited rawhide, suppled with tallow, round and smooth, and tough as steel wire, with a loop for the slip noose plaited into it at one end—a handsome rope. Whirlwind took hold of the rope below the hand of the Mandan and cut it in two between their hands, and said, "Friend, this is your horse. There is no string to this gift. I give you this pony freely, 'on the prairie,' to show that I mean what I say. Fear

nothing!" When a Cheyenne gave "on the prairie," he expected no return.

Then Killer stroked the face of his host, and thanked him, and said, "My friend, I have nothing to give you here. But I have ponies at home. They are all yours. Come to my lodge, eat, and smoke."

Whirlwind relied, "Good! Next summer when the bunchgrass is knee high I will come."

Killer mounted the spotted pony and rode around the camp circle, singing a song of thanks for the free gift of the horse. But he was not satisfied. He feared the Sioux even bearing the pipes of peace.

CHAPTER IV

A-NU'TAH SINGS A SONG

FOR Killer the Mandan the days passed quickly in
the Cheyenne camp. Food was plenty, and the
Cheyennes feasted their guests all day long. At
night there was singing and dancing and occasional
rough horse-play to raise a laugh. From time to time
the four warrior orders—the Dog Soldiers, the Bow
String Warriors, the Red Shields, and the Fox Men
—put on the distinctive regalia of their respective
orders and paraded on horseback in columns of
fours, riding at a walk around the great circle of
tipis inside and out, singing the songs of their orders. Daily there was gambling with the hoop and
sticks, with the moccasin game, and the hand game.

47

At all these the Mandan was expert. It seemed that his luck had turned when he reached the Cheyenne camp. The stakes were high and he won much property, not only from the Cheyennes, but from the Arapahos, their allies, who camped with them. With the pony Whirlwind had given him he also won races, hiring a boy to ride for him. From all these winnings he made presents freely, so that he made many friends. It a pleasant time for the Mandan.

He spent a great deal of time resting in the tipi of the chief, waiting for his leg to knit more soundly. Often A-nu'tah sat there also, busy with her household tasks. She was a handsome woman. Killer could not keep his eyes off her. He thought sourly of the old hag who waited in his lodge by the Missouri, and of how the people at home would laugh if he went courting there again. A-nu'tah was attractive. The Cheyennes were a neat and cleanly people. Their women understood the art of garnishing buffalo robes and garments with dyed porcupine quills and straw and feathers of many colors, and their clothing was far more beautiful than that of the Mandans. The technique of their domestic arts was not left to individuals, but was perpetuated by guilds to which all good housewives belonged, organizations which maintained high standards in design and execution. Killer recognized their superiority, because the women of his village merely smeared their robes with earth—red, or black, or blue—and had no skill in design.

A-nu'tah Sings a Song

One afternoon as he rested in the tipi watching A-nu'tah, she sang a song under her breath. She was sitting with downcast eyes, embroidering with deft, quick fingers a pair of leggins for Whirlwind. Killer touched her to attract her attention. Then he said, in the language of signs, "What are you singing?"

Then A-nu'tah laid aside her work and answered, "The words of the song are, *'Why do you run after me? My man is fond of me!'*" They spoke in the silent language of signs, so that no one would know. For the old mother of Whirlwind who sat in the lodge was blind.

Then Killer said to A-nu'tah, "Come with me. I am a great man among the Mandans."

A-nu'tah had been thinking of her girlhood, of how Whirlwind had seen that she was young and pretty and had come bringing presents to her father, saying, "Give me your daughter to wife." Then she had said to her father, "Do not give me to that old bear! I cannot love him. Give me to some young man." But her father had answered, "You are young and foolish. Whirlwind is a great chief. There is always meat in his tipi. Already he has three wives, and your work in his lodge will be easy. Morever, he has given me four spotted ponies with new buffalo robes tied upon their backs, and I am a poor man. Besides, I dare not refuse him. If I do, his kinsmen will come and take away you and the ponies too." So she had gone to live in the lodge of Whirlwind.

But when the Mandan said to her, "Come with

49

me," A-nu'tah was afraid. She knew what became of Cheyenne wives who were false to their husbands. The tribal standard of wifely honor was a high one, and the penalty for its violation correspondingly great. A-nu'tah had been well treated. There could be no excuse for her, if she ran away. Besides, she knew that there was no chance of escaping from the camp. Therefore A-nu'tah said nothing, and went steadily on with her work, laying the bright quills evenly upon the soft-tanned buckskin. But Killer saw that she was thinking of what he had said. He went out to water his ponies, smiling to himself. He could wait.

That day the Sioux broke camp for the first day's march towards the Cheyenne village. For several days before they had been very busy in preparation for this journey—the men freshening and repairing their warbonnets and regalia, to make the best possible appearance in the camp of their new allies,— the women packing parfleches and bags, repairing saddles and travois, making and mending moccasins and garments, and renovating all their robes with a rubbing of white clay.

In a lone tipi in the midst of the camp circle the priest and his assistants had been engaged in invoking the Mysterious Powers which direct the ceremony of the Calumet Dance, and in preparing the sacred calumets, the rattles, the wildcat skin, the perfect ear of corn ("Mother Corn"), and all other objects necessary to the performance of this holy rite.

The Calumet Dance expressed the highest spiritual and moral conceptions of the Indian race. In its teachings morality and religion met and embraced. It rose above the polytheistic worship of the people, recognized a Supreme Being, and taught the brotherhood of man with a beauty of symbolism and a loftiness of thought unparalleled in the records of primitive religion. It recognized tribal distinctions only to obliterate them. It held a pure idealism above the bloody tangle of savage life. No other ceremony was so widely spread in America as this one; no other so universally revered.

The Calumet Dance was believed to bring increase, plenty, and long life to those who joined in the ceremony. It was a beautiful and elaborate ritual, and included, as the principal event, the adoption of the chief of one tribe by the chief of another. Thus it established, with all the authority of an unquestioned religion, a supernatural blood-bond between the leaders, and so between the people, of two tribes. No obligation was held so binding as this ceremony, once it had been completed. No object was considered so sacred as the calumet. No warrior, however reckless, ever dared lay hands upon the bearers of the calumets, who passed unmolested through the territory of their most malignant foes. The whole spirit of the Calumet Dance breathed peace, goodwill to men. The Sioux were now on their way to make this ceremony with their old enemies, the Cheyennes, thus to conclude a lasting peace.

Early in the morning Ironshirt, chief of the Sioux, mounted his horse and rode swiftly around the great circle of tipis, shouting his commands and urging the people to prepare for the march. Soon after, the Sioux began to move out of the camp and away to the south. It was but a two days' march to the Cheyenne camp, so the tipis were left standing, with a sufficient guard to protect them and the aged and ailing who remained behind.

Before dawn, the priest of the ceremony had erected a tall pole in the middle of the camp. Upon this, high in the air, were exposed the calumets and other sacred objects, so that the first rays of the rising sun might vivify them for their holy mission. After sunrise the old man took these down and distributed them among his assistants, who were to carry them on the journey. He then led the way and assigned each one his place at the head of the procession.

The dignified old man was anointed with red paint and wore in his hair the downy feather of an eagle. His leggings and moccasins were clean and new. Tied about his waist with a rope of braided buffalo hair he wore a buffalo robe with the hairy side out, in token of his sacred office. In his hand he carried the perfect ear of corn—"Mother Corn"— symbol of the fruitfulness of the earth, wrapped in the skin of a wildcat. For Mother Corn was to lead the way on this journey of blessing. To the Indian the wildcat was the personification of silent, tactful success. Therefore the skin of this animal was used in this ceremony of peace and good will, from which all things warlike were excluded.

On either side of the old priest rode an athletic young man chosen for his skill and grace in dancing. On his head each wore a graceful ornament called *pe-sá*, a roachlike crest of stiff hair trimmed with eagle feathers. Each was naked except for his moccasins and the robe about his loins, and carried in his right hand, held straight before him, one of the calumets—a straight ash pipestem somewhat longer than his arm, with a shapely red stone bowl, painted and decorated in a peculiar and effective manner with beaks and feathers of birds, tufts of horsehair, and pendants white and red. These by their arrangement suggested to the Indian mind the meaning of the ceremony. To this pipestem were attached a number of the long tail feathers of the eagle, spread like a fan, and so fastened that they swayed gracefully with every movement of the bearer of the calumet, suggesting the wings of an eagle. The young athletes who carried these feathered pipes never permitted them to touch the horses. They handled them carefully at all times.

Behind these rode Ironshirt, the chief who was to adopt the Cheyenne chief in concluding the treaty. On his heels followed a group of the old men of the tribe, wearing whitened robes and carrying pipes and eagle-wing fans.

Some distance behind these the young men and mature warriors of the Sioux rode abreast in parties of ten to fifty, proceeding at a slow, regular pace, singing war songs to the accompaniment of their rattles shaken in unison. All wore their finest war dresses. Ablaze with color, shining with paint and the glitter of metal ornaments, their swaying head-dresses a-flutter with the feathers of the golden eagle and swinging ermine pendants, they made an imposing spectacle. Scalps swung from the war-clubs, lances, and shields with which they were armed. Many carried guns, though all wore at their backs fringed and embroidered quivers as well. All rode their best horses, and the animals, conscious that something unusual was afoot, pranced and champed their bits with all the spirit of the summer morning. The horses were painted in a manner which displayed the war record of their masters to every knowing eye. Many were richly caparisoned with housings of cougar skin or saddle cloths worked with quills and beads, heavily fringed, and stained with native dyes. Scalps dangled from the

bits of their Spanish bridles or from scarlet breast-straps, and many wore feathers in their tied-up tails—proof of their prowess in racing or on the war-path. Both men and horses seemed fully conscious of their war-like appearance and marched along with great dignity. But at intervals the young men ceased their singing and ran races. Then they would form again and proceed as before.

Behind came the pack train, keeping no sort of order and scattered all over the prairie for a mile and more in the rear. The women and their half-naked, bright-eyed children rode astraddle, perched high upon the heavy packs of the overburdened horses or bundled into the basket of a travois together with baggage of all sorts, dried meat, household utensils, and a litter of puppies. Beside the pack horses labored miserable, overloaded, starving dogs dragging miniature travois or bearing packs upon their sagging backs, without spirit to pursue the jack-rabbits which flashed across their path or to yelp at the squat prairie-dogs which impudently flirted their tails at their sorry namesakes before diving into the holes.

All these animals were loaded with kettles, ammunition, and pipes of red catlinite, besides woolen cloth and other goods obtained from the white traders to the east. These the Sioux wished to trade for the garnished robes of the Cheyennes and for the fine horses taken on their long raids into Mexico.

Among all these people, riding and afoot, singing, shouting, and laughing, some lost colt would run

wildly about calling its mother, or a runaway pack
horse, its load awry and spilling things at every
step, would gallop along pursued by some old hag
screaming threats and abuse after it. Dogs of every
description prowled about, now sniffing eagerly at
the hole of some creature of the prairie, now fighting savagely together, snarling, leaping, and snapping like their wolvish forebears.

Every few hours, Ironshirt, the chief, rode at full
speed back and forth through the cavalcade, giving
his orders in a loud voice. The people would then
halt, unload the horses, and rest, while the old men
sat in a circle on the grass, smoking and talking together. At such times, too, the priest and his musicians sang the sacred Songs of the Journey which
belonged to the Calumet Dance, and the calumets
were ceremonially laid to rest against a little scaffold erected for the purpose.

These halts gave the horses a rest and allowed
stragglers to catch up with the main body. When
four pipes had been smoked and the people had
rested sufficiently, Ironshirt would mount his white
war horse and gallop about shouting the order for
the start. When all were ready, he gave the order to
march, and the people proceeded as before.

At sunset camp was made near a wide pool of
water in the middle of a gently rolling plain starred
with wild flowers, across which the far-off Big Horn
Mountains loomed like a thundercloud. The old
men sat calmly smoking in the afterglow, their
white robes about their knees, while the women

unloaded, turned loose the pack animals, and prepared the evening meal. The tired horses rolled on the fresh sod or grazed beside the quiet water, while the wolf-like dogs roved everywhere through the huddled camp, searching for something to stay the pangs of their perennial hunger. In a few minutes hundreds of fires of buffalo chips were sending thin white columns of smoke into the calm evening air, while Ironshirt galloped through the encampment, jumping his horse over fires and baggage, shouting to the warriors to be alert and prevent surprise during the night. For this was the country of the Crow Indians, and they would resent the presence of the Sioux. After supper, when it began to grow dark, groups of young men left the gathering and went off in different directions to keep watch for the enemy, while the main body settled as best they could among the piles of baggage and the feet of the restless horses for the night's sleep. Nothing disturbed them. All night the solemn stars wheeled overhead in the velvet sky, while the wolves howled and yelped from the hilltops, trying to express what to them was the meaning of the vastness, the darkness, and the emptiness of the plains.

The day of the last march dawned bright and clear. At daybreak all were alert. One Horn, the old father of Ironshirt, wearing his white-tanned buffalo robe and carrying his eagle-wing fan, rode about the camp, repeating the orders of the chief, and in a short time the people had packed and were ready to start. The country was broken here for a few miles, and the young men advanced in a formation resembling a hollow square, the women riding in the middle. For in such country the Crows could cut off stragglers with impunity.

Early in the day they were met by messengers from the Cheyenne camp, and soon after halted to dress for their entry into the village of their new allies. The old men rode about haranguing at great length, urging one and all to dress carefully and look like such warriors as the Sioux were known to be. This gratuitous advice was followed to the letter. The young men mixed colored earths with tallow and anointed their faces and bodies with the greatest care. They brushed their long glossy hair smooth with a brush made from the tail of a porcupine and rubbed it with bear's grease and vermilion until it fairly shone. From buckskin bags they took out war shirts fringed with scalp-locks and worked with bright-colored quills, moccasins heavily fringed and beaded, leggings of the softest buckskin, with long, twisted fringes and broad strips of quill-work down the seams. Shields were uncovered, warbonnets shaken out and put on. All regalia of furs, feathers, and metal was arranged to the best advantage. Even the horses were painted anew with daubs of red, yellow, and blue in spots, bands, and stripes laid on in a way to blazon the brave deeds of their masters. No pains were spared, and fully two hours were consumed at the toilettes of these men of valor.

When all were ready, Ironshirt threw his painted

robe across the back of his spirited white horse and mounted. The animal was painted with a red crescent upon the breast and the red print of a man's hand upon either thigh. It had been trained to obey the pressure of its master's knees and heels, and the young chief rode without either saddle or bridle. Ironshirt wore the coat of Spainish chain mail (from which he took his name) under a handsome white war shirt of mountain sheep skin. His moccasins and leggings were beautifully embroidered with porcupine quills and heavily fringed with scalp-locks. At his back he carried a fine quiver of panther skin and a shield displaying the Thunder Bird striking lightning at his enemies. On his head he wore the horned bonnet reserved for war chiefs. As he rode through the camp at full speed, leaping his horse over baggage and camp equipage, shouting his orders and brandishing the feathered lance-banner of the Strong Hearts, the tail of his war-bonnet sweeping backward over the haunches of his horse almost to the ground, he was the admiration of every woman and the envy of every young man in the tribe. Ironshirt was brave in battle, generous to the poor and helpless, and universally beloved by his people.

He was feared as well by his enemies. The iron shirt which he wore was believed to have wonderful powers as a war medicine. The chief had obtained it by barter from the Kiowas years before, and ever since it had protected its owner in battle and brought him out victorious in every skirmish. He

had never been wounded. For he had carefully followed all the directions given him by the man from
whom he had bought the shirt. The Kiowa knew all
about such matters, for they had had a number of
these coats of mail, captured or obtained in other
ways from the Spaniards whom they had met on the
southern plains. The Sioux chief diligently observed
the obligatory tabus and customs in which the protective power of the shirt was believed to reside. As
a result, he had been invincible and invulnerable.

At his command the women took their stations,
the young men mounted, and the whole party
moved off together. The proud warriors rode as
stiffly as their restive horses would allow, and took
great care to protect their finery. No more races
were run. All were singing. Thus they advanced
over the rolling prairie beyond whose gentle swells
lay the Cheyenne camp.

Ironshirt and the keepers of the calumet rode
abreast in front, while all the others formed a long
line at their heels, like a troop of cavalry passing in
review. Behind this long line rode the women some
distance in the rear. As the Sioux came over the last
hilltop overlooking the camp, they saw the line of
the Cheyenne warriors advancing to meet them
at a slow walk. At once the Sioux halted. The Cheyennes continued to advance, singing their war songs
and shaking their rattles in unison, and breaking
out at intervals into a chorus of wolflike yelps. They
came to a halt at last at a distance of about fifty
paces. All the men of both parties continued singing

and shouting and shaking their rattles, while their horses, meeting thus suddenly, became much excited, neighed, and pranced, adding to the uproar and confusion.

The Cheyennes were outnumbered by the Sioux, but their horses were much better. Many of these were beautiful, spirited animals, descendants of the Arabs brought to Mexico by the Spaniards. They were all well built and active, though smaller than their ancestors—the horses stolen from or lost by the adventurous Spanish cavaliers who rode northwards in a vain search for the fabulous golden cities of Cibola. The hard winters of the plains had toughened them, but at the same time had diminished the size of the breed. Many of the horses were masked in a startling fashion to imitate the head of a buffalo, antelope, or deer, with natural skin and horns intact, the eyes, mouth, and nostrils of the mask being trimmed with red cloth. The masks gave them a most ferocious appearance.

Few of the Cheyennes had guns, and these were mostly poor ones. They lived too far to the west to

profit much by trade with the white men. Their country was full of beaver, but they did not know how to trap them nor where to dispose of them. They had few articles of white man's manufacture. Otherwise their costumes were not greatly different from those of the Sioux.

Suddenly Whirlwind dashed out from among his warriors and rode at a gallop towards the Sioux. Naked save for breechcloth and moccasins, he wore on his head a superb doublt-tail warbonnet of eagle feathers which swept the ground on either side his horse. At his back he carried a quiver, and in his hand a lance. His shield bore the device of a buffalo bull's head. Over his right shoulder trailed the long leather sash which marked him as a chief of the Dog Soldiers, most powerful of the Cheyenne warrior orders. His beautiful black mount was caparisoned with a quill-worked leather saddlecloth, and its tail and mane were decorated with eagle feathers.

Whirlwind rode at full speed directly up to Iron-shirt, pulled his mount to a sudden standstill, and embraced the Sioux chief in the saddle with all the grace and ease of the born horseman. In like manner he then embraced the old priest, the two bearers of the calumets, and the chiefs. Then he turned to the line of warriors and embraced individuals here and there, making them welcome to the Cheyenne camp in a cordial and affable manner.

Immediately the whole body of Cheyenne warriors charged the Sioux at top speed and at the same moment the Sioux advanced at a gallop. Every Cheyenne selected some Sioux for his comrade, embraced him, and rode by his side towards the camp, with every sign of friendly welcome. As the warriors swept towards the camp, Ironshirt and Whirlwind rode at full speed through the ranks, shouting instructions to their people, telling them to be friendly, to welcome each other, and to forget all former hatreds.

At the entrance to the camp the warriors thus mingled together formed in column of fours with the calumets in the lead and marched at a walk around the great circle of tipis, inside and out, singing as they went. Then, entering the camp again, they formed in the center and remained there singing until the women had reached the camp and unsaddled at the tipis into which they were invited. The formation then broke up and the Sioux warriors were conducted into the tipis of the Cheyennes.

Meanwhile, the chiefs and old men rode through the camp, shouting their commands, urging their people to feed the guests well, to play no foolish

pranks, and to make a firm and lasting peace between the two nations.

There was feasting everywhere. Hour after hour men could be heard calling their friends and guests to "come, eat, and smoke," in their tipis. The Sioux women were busy exchanging their wares for the garnished robes and dressed leather of the Cheyennes. Each woman, anxious to dispose of her property to the best advantage, carried a load from tipi to tipi around the circle. But the Sioux so outnumbered their hosts that the market was overstocked, and many of the women were forced to keep what they had brought.

When the Sioux warriors came into the camp, Killer the Mandan left the painted tipi and lay down in one of the other lodges of his host. For Whirlwind had three lodges because of his many wives. Killer knew that the chief would be feasting the Sioux in his finest tipi, and he had no mind to meet the Sioux until after the Calumet Dance had been completed. Moreover, his leg hurt him, as he told the women in the lodge.

Now when the formation broke up, Whirlwind brought Ironshirt to his tipi and spoke to the women. Then one of them spread a robe for the guest to sit upon, and another placed food before him in a wooden bowl, while a third kindled a fire in the kitchen and put on a brass kettle to cook meat. Quickly the lodge was cleared of household stuff. Robes were spread round the lodge for seats, and a small fire was built in the center.

Whirlwind stood before the door of his tipi and called in the manner of a crier, naming the principal men of the Cheyennes and the Sioux and asking them to come to his feast in honor of Ironshirt. The Cheyenne chief had been greatly honored in being chosen for the Son in the Calumet Dance, the chief who was to be adopted. He wished to show his appreciation of this honor by feasting the man who had thus complimented him.

While the women were cooking the food for the feast, it happened that certain Sioux warriors passed the kitchen. They were thirsty and stopped to ask for a drink of water that hung in a paunch in the shade there. Among them was One Horn, the old father of Ironshirt, and Two Crows, a chief. The women gave them the paunch, and each one drank in turn. When One Horn smelled the good stew cooking in the kettle, he was tempted, and took the iron spoon that lay there and helped himself. But his hand shook so that the hot broth was spilled and fell upon his bare legs and burned him. He dropped the spoon into the kettle and it sank to the bottom. They all laughed at the old man's accident, and the women offered him a spoon of ram's-horn with which to dip up the stew. But One Horn had had enough. The old man went away with the others, laughing and gesticulating over his accident. The iron spoon remained in the kettle.

When the guests had assembled at Whirlwind's tipi, they all sat down upon the robes around the fire, talking and laughing together. Everyone

looked forward with pleasure to the coming ceremony and the lasting peace that was to follow. Presently the women brought the brass kettle filled with
meat and handed it through the doorway of the
lodge, passing in the spoon of ram's-horn after. Two
young men who sat near the door stood up and
carried the kettle around the lodge, serving every
man with the good stew. Whirlwind did not eat,
for the feast was in his tipi.

Ironshirt and Two Crows sat with the others and
ate the stew that was in the kettle. One Horn, the
father of Ironshirt, was not present, having been
asked to feast in another tipi. When the guests had
emptied their bowls, the young men carried the
kettle around the circle again, and every man
helped himself. As he dipped in the kettle, one of
the guests found the iron spoon in the bottom and
took it out, and showed it, laughing. For he had
thought it was a bone he was getting. When the
others understood, they laughed too.

Then Ironshirt said to his friend Two Crows,
"That breaks my medicine."

Ironshirt's protective charm was broken if he ate
food touched by an iron tool. His coat of mail would
protect him only if all the tabus and obligatory
customs were observed, and this was one of them.
He knew that his medicine was broken. But One
Horn, his father, knew nothing about this, though
he was the cause of it. Two Crows did not tell Ironshirt that his own father had broken his medicine.

For Two Crows felt to blame in the matter himself, now that he remembered the incident.

While the guests were eating, Whirlwind carefully filled the red stone bowl of his long-stemmed pipe with tobacco and red willow bark. When all had finished, he lighted the pipe, offered smoke to the sun and earth and the four winds, and passed it to his neighbor. All the others smoked, passing the pipe from hand to hand around the circle. Whirlwind was happy. From time immemorial Sioux and Cheyenne had fought one another. Now there was to be peace, and the heart of the chief was glad. He talked of the coming ceremony with enthusiasm, and made the Sioux very welcome. As they smoked he told them how his son Little Chief had killed his first buffalo. Then the Sioux praised the boy and his father was very proud.

When the feast was over and the fourth pipe had been smoked out, Whirlwind cleaned the ashes from the pipe bowl and said, "It is finished." The guests departed, carrying their bowls, singing songs of thanks in honor of their host. But Ironshirt and Two Crows were worried because Ironshirt had broken his medicine.

Feasting went on merrily and gaiety prevailed everywhere in the camp. The Sioux found themselves going from tipi to tipi to feast, until they had to carry away in their bowls the food they could not eat. Social dances were organized. Warrior orders paraded. Young men competed in horse racing and in gambling of all kinds. The women bartered and gambled, tossing the dice in the basket, while their wrinkled mothers sat by smoking their short pipes and laughing at every lucky turn of the play. Children splashed in the pools of the creek beside the camp. The young men were continually on horseback, riding around the circle of tipis, singing together, two and sometimes three on one horse to show their good feeling. Parties of Sioux walked round the circle singing begging-songs and halting before the tipi of every prominent man to dance until he acknowledged the compliment with a gift of food or ponies. Everyone was happy.

Meanwhile, Cheyenne women had erected in the center of the camp circle a large shelter in which the Calumet Dance was to take place. This shelter was made of the smoke-stained coverings of six large tipis supported upon tipi poles thrust vertically into the ground, the whole forming a semi-circle opening towards the entrance of the camp. All round within this shelter to a height of six feet were stretched additional coverings, similar to those used to canopy beds in a tipi. Behind the place of honor opposite the doorway, a great buffalo robe painted with a device representing the sun was hung up. A small fire was built in the center of the shelter.

Those of Ironshirt's party—the Fathers of the ceremony of adoption—now joined with the Sons—the party of Whirlwind—in preparing the shelter for the dance. A rectangle was outlined on the turf near the fire, the sod was loosened, and the earth dug up, in order that the beneficent influence of Mother Earth might be felt. Behind this cleared spot, on a bed of fresh wild sage, a bleached buffalo skull, picked up on the prairie and painted with mystic symbols, was laid nose to the fire. Back of the skull was set up the little scaffold against which the calumets were to rest when not in use. Behind this, and just in front of the seat of the priest of the ceremony, was laid the tobacco pouch and pipe for the burnt offering. Here too were placed the braided sweetgrass used for incense, the pouch of red paint and sponge of buffalo wool used in painting the face of the Son with the red paint—symbol of God's love for man. When this had been done, the singers took their seats around the large decorated drum to one side of the skull. The dance lodge was ready for the calumets.

Whirlwind entered the dance lodge and took his seat near the door in the humblest place. It was a great honor the Sioux had done him in choosing him from all his nation to be the adopted Son in this ceremony. But he did not seek his own honor, only the good of his people.

Presently the priest with his assistants and the two dancers carrying the calumets came and halted at the entrance, singing the sacred song. And when the Song of the Threshold had been sung, the priest passed into the dance lodge and took his seat in the place of honor behind the buffalo skull, facing the entrance. He spread the wildcat skin before him and thrust the point of the stick which supported

Mother Corn into the ground nearby. Ironshirt and his party found seats around the lodge.

At once the musicians about the drum began tapping it with steady rhythm. Soon after, the two dancers laid aside their robes and began to dance, waving the calumets to the cadence of the music. They were fine, athletic figures, and stepped in perfect time to the rhythm of the drum, shaking in unison the rattles held in their left hands. They were nude save for their moccasins and long red breech-clouts of woolen cloth. Their only ornament was the roachlike crest of stiff hair trimmed with eagle feathers which they wore upon their heads. They passed completely round the dance lodge while the musicians sang the Song of the Mother Eagle, waving the calumets as an eagle waves her wings, bending and swaying their lithe young bodies with all the grace of a soaring bird.

Four times they danced around the lodge, the musicians singing one stanza for each circuit. In the first stanza the Mother Eagle was represented as hovering far above the lodge, as an eagle hovers above her nest high in the air. In the second stanza she was represented as flying down into the lodge as an eagle flies down to her nest. In the third stanza she was represented as cleansing the lodge of all evil, as an eagle cleanses her nest, sweeping it outward and away with mighty wings. In the fourth stanza the Mother Eagle was represented as settling upon the lodge, as an eagle settles upon her nest. The eagle is from above, and in this ceremony she represents the Love of the Power that is above. That was the meaning of the song.

As they made these circuits while the musicians sang and beat upon the drum, the two young men danced in imitation of the flight of an eagle, waving the calumets as an eagle waves her wings, for the feathers of the eagle were fastened upon the calumets to give the appearance of wings. So the dancers waved the calumets as a mother eagle waves her wings when she hovers, and when she flies down, and when she cleanses her nest, and when she settles upon it. That was the meaning of the dance. No other ceremony was so beautiful; no other music so pleasing; no other dance so graceful. Thus the lodge was dedicated to the ceremony of the Calumet Dance.

When the Song of the Mother Eagle had been sung, the dancers laid the calumets against the scaffold behind the buffalo skull and seated themselves near the priest. Then Ironshirt took the bundle of fine clothing he had brought and went to Whirlwind. He made him remove the garments he had on and put on the new things the Sioux had made for his new Son. These were beautiful, finely made, and embroidered—moccasins, leggings, and shirt of the softest buckskin, fringed and painted, and over all a fine soft buffalo robe with a great ornament representing the sun. Then Whirlwind thanked the Sioux chief and embraced him, and gave away his old clothing to poor at the door. For he had long desired to have peace with the Sioux, and his heart was glad.

The old men now harangued the camp, calling the people to the dance lodge to see the ceremony. They quickly gathered about the lodge and crowded together to see what was being done and to admire the fine gifts which had been made. Everyone was happy to see the ceremony under way. They were all glad to be at peace and their hearts were singing.

When Killer the Mandan heard the old men harangue the camp and saw the people rushing to the lodge to see the Calumet Dance, he thought that his chance had come to get a little air and water his ponies. He was tired of staying in the stuffy little tipi where the chief's worn-out wives lived together. He wrapped a Cheyenne robe about him so that his face and hair were concealed. Only his eyes were visible. He went out after his ponies, took their lariats in his free hand, and mounted one of them. Then he rode down to the little stream, leading his horses.

It was inconvenient to manage them muffled up in his robe. But he would not let them run loose. For he thought that, if he had to ride for his life, he would want his ponies ready at hand. The ponies waded into the shallows and drank, swinging their wet muzzles backwards to sweep off troublesome flies, snapping and squealing at one another, pawing and splashing in the water, and switching their tails vigorously. They had been tied up all day and were full of spirit.

As Killer sat there, waiting for the playful ponies to finish their drinking, holding their lariats in his right hand and grasping his robe with the other, suddenly two boys came by, racing their ponies along the bank of the little stream. As they passed, Killer's ponies threw up their heads and started after them. The lariats tautened as they moved away, and, feeling the pull of the ropes, they swung around, one one way, another another, so that the Mandan could not manage them and became entangled in the ropes.

The boys laughed at his predicament, and rode by again to excite his ponies still more. The boys thought it was some old man, and they loved a joke. Certainly, they thought, a man who rides out on a summer's day muffled to the eyes in a hot robe deserves a misfortune! They rode by again at the gallop, shouting and waving their arms to frighten the ponies.

Meanwhile, the priest of the Calumet Dance was filling the pipe for the burnt offering of tobacco. This pipe was to be smoked by the two principals of the ceremony—Ironshirt, the ceremonial Father; Whirlwind, the ceremonial Son. The smoking of this pipe together was the first binding step in the Calumet Dance. It was believed that the smoke of such an offering carried their prayers to the Great Mystery and pledged them under penalty of His displeasure to love and serve one another. Henceforth they must be as father and son. The smoking of this pipe was therefore not a matter to be undertaken lightly or in haste, and the ritual allowed time for meditation and prayer at this point. Even now either of the two parties might draw back and put an end to the ceremony. When the pipe was ready, the old priest rose from his place behind the calumets and slowly carried it to Whirlwind.

The Cheyenne chief received the pipe from the old man, who went back to his place. Whirlwind held it reverently in his hand, and sat thinking of the seriousness of this step, while the musicians struck up the first movement of the grave old Song of Counsel—

"Give heed, my son! Pray!"

Holding the pipe in his hand, Whirlwind thought how long years before the Cheyennes had been peaceful farmers, living in log houses and raising corn and beans in the rich bottoms along the Missouri. They were a small tribe, and the Sioux, in their great westward migration, had driven them away from the river and out upon the plains, where agriculture was impossible and every man's hand was against them. They had lost their seed corn. Even the tobacco, so necessary for their religious rites, had ceased to be grown by them. They had followed the buffalo for a living. They had no permanent homes. Since that time they had become great fighters; they had fought many tribes. But always the Assiniboine Sioux had been their most powerful adversaries. Now there was to be peace. Whirlwind prayed earnestly that this ceremony of the calumets might unite the two tribes in a peace that would endure. He sat with bowed head, holding the pipe unlighted in his hand, while the musicians sang the last stanza of the Song of Counsel—

"Give heed, my son!"

As the boys raced past the Mandan the second time, his ponies became quite unmanageable, and broke wildly away. Their lariats were twisted around his body, and he was dragged from his horse and fell flat on his back with a great splash in the shallow water. The boys watched his struggles with delight, rocking in their saddles and shouting with laughter. But as the drenched warrior got to his feet, their laughter was turned to astonishment. Each of them unconsciously covered his mouth with his hand in token of surprise. For Killer had lost his robe in his fall, and the arrangement of his hair at once betrayed the Mandan.

When he gained his feet, Killer saw at once that he was discovered. He quickly scrambled out of the water and ran towards his pony which had stopped at no great distance. For a moment the boys stood motionless, frozen with astonishment. Then with one accord they quirted their ponies and rushed the Mandan, giving the war cry. For they were both Sioux. But Killer evaded them and caught his pony, mounted it, and rode hard towards the entrance to the camp.

75

The boys pursued, yelling and calling to others nearby, who joined in the chase. Others came running from all sides, both Cheyennes and Sioux, and gathered about Killer, blocking his way to the camp, shouting and gesticulating excitedly. The Sioux tried to force their horses into the crowd to strike the Mandan. The Cheyennes were trying to explain that the stranger was their guest and must not be molested.

When this outcry was heard at the dance lodge, the men there left the dance and came running and riding with their weapons to see what the trouble might be. A great crowd collected about the unlucky Mandan and pressed upon him so that he could not stir. He was almost naked and armed only with the knife in his belt. He knew that his safety rested with the small group of Cheyennee warriors gathered about him, for he could not fight his way out of such a mob. Bloodshed was the last thing he wanted, under the circumstances.

At first, all was confusion. But very soon the matter was understood, and the situation became more threatening. The leading warriors of the Sioux had arrived and began shouting that the Mandan must not enter the camp, that they would kill him where he stood. The Cheyennes tried to explain to them that the Mandan was their guest, and were keeping the noisy Sioux away from him as best they could, though the pressure of the crowd was momentarily becoming greater and harder to cope with. The confusion grew with every second; the crowd swayed back and forth, and a great cloud of dust rose above it. The Cheyennes were so outnumbered that they could make no headway in their efforts to get the Mandan into camp. The Sioux realized their power and pushed and shouted, trying to get at the cause of the commotion.

Meanwhile, the Sioux women, hearing the uproar, made haste to catch up and load their pack horses. All worked as fast as possible, scowling and in silence, without any of that bawling and garrulous chatter usual among them when packing. No one waited to ask what the trouble was. In a very few minutes the Sioux women were ready to march.

When Whirlwind heard the uproar and saw the men running towards the entrance to the camp, he took the pipe and reverently carried it to the old priest on his seat behind the calumets. Then he left the dance lodge. Ironshirt and the others had already gone. Whirlwind jumped on a horse and rode

at full speed to the scene of the trouble. He thrust his horse into the middle of the crowd, ruthlessly trampling and pushing aside those who stood in his path. In the midst of the little group of Cheyennes, mostly boys, he saw Killer. The Mandan, dripping wet and smeared with the dust that had blown upon his damp skin and hair, sat his pony, nervously looking from side to side with bright, excited eyes, breathing hard, his hand on the haft of the knife in his belt. The Sioux all about him pushed and reached, striking at him with whatever they held in their hands, trying to count the coup and thereby add to their war honors. They were held at a distance by the little cordon of Cheyennes, and although an occasional lance butt or the end of an outstretched bow touched the Mandan, he could not be harmed by them.

Whirlwind realized the plight of his guest at once. Pushing his horse alongside Killer's, he took him by the hand and said, "Friend, go into the camp without fear. So long as I can hold my war-club, you have nothing to fear from the Sioux." Then the Cheyenne chief, calling upon his tribesmen for support, began to push back the Sioux and clear a path into the camp. It was only a short distance, but the stubborn Sioux grudged every inch of the way, sullenly refusing to budge from the path until pushed aside by superior force.

As the compact little body of Cheyennes about Killer began to move slowly through the dense mass of surging humanity and horseflesh, Ironshirt planted himself in the path of Whirlwind and, pushing up to him, appealed to him not to interfere in the matter, but to leave the Mandan to the Sioux to deal with. The Cheyenne chief answered, "This man has eaten in my tipi. I cannot let you kill him." But Ironshirt placed the ends of the lariats of three good horses in the hand of Whirlwind and said, "My friend, I give you these three horses. Let the Sioux have the Mandan. He is still outside the camp."

But Whirlwind turned to Killer and placed the lariats in his hand. He said, "Friend, I give you these ponies to show that I mean what I say. Let us go into the camp."

When the Sioux saw that, they were angry and began to thrust at Killer with the points of their lances, trying to reach him over the heads of the Cheyennes. Some of the young men began to sing war songs, and one or two shouted the war cry. One of them drew his bow and tried to shoot at Killer. But an old man snatched the arrow away and the chiefs called out that men must not shoot in such a crowd.

Gradually the path to the camp was cleared, the Sioux gave way, and Whirlwind brought the Mandan safely to his own tipi, invited him to enter, and placed a guard of young men about the tent. Then he quietly returned to the dance lodge. He had done his duty by his guest. Now he would do his duty by his people.

But others were not so easily satisfied. The Sioux crowded in great numbers about the tipi where

Killer was, jostling the Cheyennes there and making threats that they would kill the Mandan inside the camp the same as out. The Cheyennes were anxious to be at peace with the Sioux, but they were firm in their determination to defend their guest. The Sioux felt that the Cheyennes had slighted their friendship for one miserable Mandan—outside the camp at that, where no obligation of hospitality should be binding. Of all the prairie tribes, no people were haughtier and more sensitive than the Sioux, unless it were the Cheyennes. The Sioux felt that no one could be friendly towards them who entertained a Mandan; while the Cheyennes resented having the Sioux presume to dictate to them in their own camp.

The confusion and uproar and threats continued and grew in volume. Finally, Gray Thunder, one of the chiefs of the Dog Soldiers, mounted his horse and harangued the camp, calling together the warriors of his order. When they were assembled, he led them, singing their war songs, and surrounded the lodge where the Mandan was, driving the Sioux away and taking Killer under the protection of the Dog Soldiers. These erected a shelter for themselves nearby, and the disgruntled Sioux retired to their tipis.

Meanwhile the chiefs and old men of both tribes rode round and round the camp, shouting orders and admonitions to their people, forbidding the frightened women to decamp, as many were ready to do, and urging the men to control themselves and not start a fight which might bring on a general massacre of the women and children. The uproar and threats, the shouting and the talking did not cease until dark. When it did, the silence in the great camp was even more ominous.

Whirlwind waited in the dance lodge. He was alone except for the old priest and the keepers of the calumets. Their duties prevented them from leaving the consecrated lodge before the ceremony had been completed. Even these had nothing to say to him. They were Sioux.

No one else came near. A heavy cloud covered the sky. There were rumblings of thunder in the west. Whirlwind walked back to his tipi at sunset through a cold drizzle which settled with darkness into a steady rain.

CHAPTER V

THE END OF THE CALUMET DANCE

NEXT morning the Cheyennes, eager to conclude the treaty, gathered in force at the shelter erected for the Calumet Dance. But not a Sioux came near, for they were all sulky and sore, and sat in the tipis, taking no part in the ceremony. At last the old priest went with his assistants carrying the calumets to the tipi where Ironshirt was staying. They were all Sioux, but the priest held that the ceremony, once begun, should not be broken off. Moreover, if the treaty fell through, he and his assistants stood to lose many gifts which would otherwise be given them for their services.

When the party reached the tipi where Ironshirt

was, the musicians sang sacred songs while the bearers of the calumets danced before the lodge. This went on for some time. Nevertheless, Ironshirt would not come out. He was too angry with the Cheyennes to join in a ceremony having such an obligation. After a while, Whirlwind widened the door of the tipi by pulling out the wooden pins that fastened the lodge-covering above and below and rolling it up along the poles. The priest and his dancers entered the tipi and danced before Ironshirt, offering him the calumet. The Sioux chief gave no sign that he saw them, and sat with his head down in sullen anger. He would not take the calumet.

The priest appealed to the old men of the Sioux, haranguing them on the benefits of the ceremony and the blessings of peace between the two tribes. The old men talked at great length together and with Ironshirt, until at last, after the priest had urged him and offered him the calumet repeatedly, he took it in a careless manner and evidently much against his will. His heart was hot against the Cheyennes.

Immediately Whirlwind handed to him the lariats of three good horses. The Sioux chief turned the animals over to his wife. Then Whirlwind and another Cheyenne chief took Ironshirt by the arms and slowly led him from the tipi to the dance lodge, followed by the calumets and by crowds of Sioux and Cheyennes on foot. There they seated themselves near the buffalo skulls and the calumets were laid to rest with due ceremony against the little scaffold over the wildcat skin. The Sioux chief sat there with his head down, sore and angry.

At this point in the ceremony it was the custom to bring offerings, by way of trade, to the calumets and the buffalo skull. The wildcat skin beneath the calumets lay ready to receive the gifts of the Cheyennes, while a buffalo robe was spread near the skull to receive those of the Sioux. The criers stood without the shelter and harangued the people, each in his own language, announcing the time for bringing offerings.

At once the Cheyennes came forward with a number of richly garnished robes and fine dressed leather, smoke-tanned so as not to become stiff when wetted. These were placed upon the wildcat skins, and the Cheyennes awaited the response of the Sioux. There was a long delay. Again the criers harangued. After some time, one of the Sioux brought two old guns and placed them beside the skull. Again the Cheyennes brought forward new robes and several good horses. And again, after an even longer delay, the Sioux brought gifts—three scabby, sore-backed ponies, badly bitten by the wolves and quite worthless.

Then Whirlwind could contain himself no longer. He jumped to his feet and addressed the Sioux vehemently in their own language, bitterly reproaching them for offering their trash and rotten horses. Even good horses, he said, were nothing to the Cheyennes. They had more than they could use already, and these old crow-baits were no good. The Cheyennes, he said, were willing to offer good robes and fine horses, eagle tails and ermines, but they expected the Sioux to bring good guns and ammunition. He accompanied his words with many lively gestures so that those who could not understand the Sioux tongue could readily follow him. Then he sat down.

To all this the Sioux made no reply for a long time. They talked among themselves apart from the Cheyennes. No more offerings were forthcoming. At last, one of their old men proposed gravely that, if the Cheyennes would place all their guns and ammunition on the wildcat skin, the Sioux would then bring their own weapons to the skull.

At once the Cheyennes scented treachery. It was contrary to the custom of the ceremony to specify the gifts to be offered, and this brazen proposal made the Cheyennes believe that the wily Sioux were planning to disarm them and wipe them out. They had only a few guns, while the Sioux had many. Outnumbered as they were, it would be little better than suicide to give up their arms.

Whirlwind got up, drew his robe about him, and blandly suggested, with a sardonic smile, that the Sioux bring their own guns first. But the Sioux would not respond to this. So matters stood. Neither side would make any concessions. The Sioux were haughtily offended that the Cheyennes could prefer the life of a paltry Mandan to their friendship; the Cheyennes were determined to protect their guest at all hazards and to endure no more insults and insolence from the Sioux.

The old priest tried to bring the two leaders together again. But Ironshirt would not smoke with Whirlwind, and when the pipe was offered to him, the Cheyenne chief rose from his seat and left the dance lodge. In a few moments the crowd had melted away. The two parties returned to their tipis, taking their gifts with them. The priest and his assistants took the calumets and departed. Cheyenne women removed the shelter. By noon the spot was deserted. The Calumet Dance had come to an end.

During the afternoon the feeling in camp became very tense. The prairie Sioux were among the proudest and haughtiest of men, bearing themselves with a lordly assurance which marked them off from most of the tribes of the plains. No less

remarkable for headstrong temper and desperate courage, pride of bearing and tenacity of purpose, were the Cheyennes—men pre-eminently warriors among a people whose trade was war. These two tribes, huddled together in the same camp, sharing the same tipis, eating and sleeping together and at the same time cherishing such hatred and smoldering resentment as now, could scarcely fail sooner or later to clash with fatal results. The Cheyennes were eager to show their prowess and courage, outnumbered though they were. The Sioux were equally content to quarrel and eager to avenge the slight to their calumets. Many threats passed between the young men of the two tribes, and the women vented their petty spite upon each other as best they could. Cheyenne hosts looked aside when their guests entered the tipi. Trade was at an end. There was no more feasting or crying of feasts. The warriors no longer paraded together, or sat smoking and talking over old battles and feats of hunting. The women's games of dice and ball were discontinued. The young men no longer raced their ponies over the prairie, but kept them picketed close to the lodges, awaiting the strife which they felt sure would come. The camp was quiet with an ominous silence, broken only by the neighing of horses, the howling of dogs, and the harangues of the old men. Only the desire to protect the women and children from indiscriminate massacre prevented immediate battle.

It was very hot and sultry in that corner of the hills. The people, heated by the excitement of the morning, were very thirsty. In every tipi hung the paunch of a buffalo filled with water. But whenever a Sioux stretched out his hand for a drink, some Cheyenne snatched the water away. The little creek nearby was almost dry, and its standing pools had been so fouled by the hundreds of horses about the camp that no human being could drink the water. As things stood, it was unsafe for a Sioux woman to go all the way to the river for water. So the Sioux sweltered and thirsted, and their anger grew the hotter.

One of the Sioux out looking after his ponies happened to meet a Cheyenne woman returning from the river with a paunch of fresh water on her shoulders. She saw him coming and guessed his thought. He knew that she would refuse him, if he asked for water. So he snatched the paunch from her hands, cut it open, and drank his fill. At once the woman began to struggle with him for the possession of the paunch, setting up a shrill cry that brought the Cheyennes swarming from their tipis. The Sioux also caught up their weapons and came running in large numbers. In a moment a great crowd had collected around the woman and the Sioux warrior, and immediate battle threatened.

There was no shouting, only a silent, angry truculence far more menacing. But before the storm broke, Ironshirt dashed up on his white war horse, took the paunch from his rash follower and restored it to the woman. Then he drove the unlucky warrior back to his tipi, beating him savagely over the head and naked shoulders with a quirt. This summary discipline somewhat mollified the anger of the Cheyennes over the incident and gave warning to the Sioux that their chief would tolerate no fighting in the camp, angry though he was. Ironshirt wanted no battle there, where the women and children must suffer terribly, no matter how the fight turned out. He saw it was high time to go, for any trifle might mean death to hundreds.

The Sioux chief rode to the center of the great circle of tipis and shouted his commands. They were instantly obeyed. The Sioux assembled about him, eager to be gone. Many of the women had packed up hours ago, and only the threats and orders of the chiefs had prevented them from slipping away before. There was the greatest hurry, bustle, and confusion. Children cried. Dogs ran everywhere, getting in people's way and being kicked for their pains. Fat old women, who could scarcely waddle along in ordinary times, now rushed about, bawling and yelling, dragging at the lead ropes of reluctant pack ponies. Horses became excited and refractory. The warriors were busy putting on their war paint and uncovering their shields, while the old men rode about haranguing and shouting. It seemed that order could never come out of that chaos. But in a very brief time all were ready, and at the word of command the women moved out of the camp in a close body and disappeared over the hill at a rapid gait.

The main body of Sioux warriors formed in the

middle of the camp. When the women had gained some distance, the men followed, riding at a slow walk in an irregular but compact formation, ready for battle, and apparently in no hurry to avoid it. Every man was painted and armed for war. Feathers fluttered in the light breeze. Scalps swayed on lance and bridle bit with the steady swing of the horses' bodies. Shields decorated with feathers, fur, and hair displayed their garish colors and conventional devices of animals and heavenly bodies. Those men who had guns carried them ready loaded, and rode with an extra bullet in the mouth. Everyone was inwardly excited, though preserving outward calm. The horses neighed and plunged, conscious of their masters' agitation. They rode away with an air of insolence, and so slowly that every Cheyenne was inflamed anew with anger.

When the Cheyennes saw the Sioux making ready to depart, the men made haste to paint themselves for war, making final preparations for the battle which they saw impending. They took their war clothing from the soft leather sacks and rawhide cases, holding the different articles to the four directions in turn, to the earth and the sun, before putting them on. Shields were slipped from their covers and their ornaments shaken free in the sunlight. With all these preparations there were prayers and much singing for protection and success in the coming fight.

Meanwhile the women were busy digging shallow rifle pits among the tipis. Soon the Cheyenne warriors began to mount and follow the Sioux, shouting many threats after them and making gestures of defiance which the Sioux affected not to notice. As the warriors rode away, the women stood beside the tipis shouting and singing to hearten them. Here and there some old mother of warriors screamed out the war whoop—that unearthly, quavering cry, the ideal expression of the passion and terror of the hunting of man.

Beside his tipi door, Seven Bulls stood leaning on his staff, his face shining with excitement. He was wrapped in his robe, and clutched his eagle-wing fan in claw-like hands. The old man could fight no longer, but his voice was like a trumpet. As the warriors rode away they could hear him calling after them. "Young men, be brave. Fight hard. Never retreat. When you get old you cannot enjoy your food. Your teeth are no good. Your legs are no good. You must sit on the cold side of the lodge. Your clothing will be made from some worn out tipi-cover. After a while you will get so feeble that you cannot travel, and the people will leave you on the prairie for the wolves to devour. It is better to die young in battle, fighting like a man, killing the enemy!"

Whirlwind had put on the uniform of a leader of the Dog Soldiers, most powerful of the Cheyenne warrior organizations. When he was ready to go, he came out of the tipi to mount his horse.

There he found his son Little Chief waiting, ready mounted, to follow him after the Sioux.

Whirlwind was troubled. Little Chief was only a boy. He had no war medicine to charm away the bullets of the Sioux. He had never fasted alone among the hills until the Mysterious Powers appeared to him and offered him help. He had never seen a skirmish. If he went into this fight, he would surely be killed. The Sioux were very many.

Whirlwind went back into the tipi and came out again with a bag of paints, a shield in its cover, a warbonnet, and a medicine pouch. These constituted his personal medicine or charm, and these he gave to his son for this fight. For the uniform of the Dog Soldiers protected him, and a leader of the Dog Soldiers carried no shield into battle.

Whirlwind's medicine was the Dragon Fly.

"My son," he said, "the dragon fly is the most deadly of all flying insects. He is swift. He never misses his prey. He hovers high over the water, but when he strikes, he kills. His enemies cannot catch him. He jumps back and forth so rapidly that they cannot touch him. You must act like him."

Then the chief took paint and anointed the face and body of Little Chief with blue, for the dragon fly is blue. On the shoulder of the boy's pony he painted a conventionalized figure of a dragon fly. Then, facing the horse towards the east, he lifted one foot after another and spat upon them the shreds of a root he was chewing.

"My son," he said, "this is the root of the plant the dragon fly likes best. This is the plant he always sits upon when he is resting. I have put this on your

93

horse's feet to make him swift and sure like the dragon fly. He will not step in the prairie-dog holes. He will be quick. The bullets will not hit him. He will be like the dragon fly."

Then the chief took his shield and stripped off the cover. The shield was large and round, of tough hide taken from the neck of a buffalo bull, shrunk and hardened by fire, and covered with a thin sheath of buckskin on which were painted a number of dragon flies surrounding a bull's head. Attached to the shield were a number of eagle feathers, scalps, and a single bear claw. All these ornaments Whirlwind shook loose. He held the shield four times towards the sky, shook it four times towards the earth, then hung it upon the boy's left arm, where a shield should be carried in battle.

"My son," he said, "this is the medicine I received

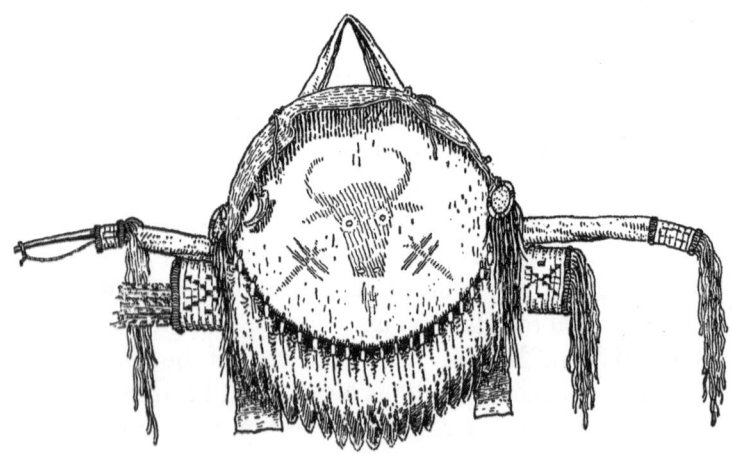

when the spirits took pity on me. There is no song to go with this shield. The dragon fly has no song. He is silent, but he never misses his prey. When you ride into battle, do not sing. Ride about swiftly here and there and kill quickly like the dragon fly.

"I want you to stay here in camp. Keep a sharp lookout. There are many Sioux. If there is a fight, some of them may try to attack the camp. If they do, fight hard. Remember that your enemies are as frightened as you are. If you see a friend in a tight place, help him. Fight hard. Then, if you are killed, the enemy will say, 'This was a brave man; he was hard to kill!' "

Finally the chief took from its cylindrical case of painted rawhide his great bonnet of eagle feathers and placed it upon the boy's head, tying the chin straps beneath the chin and the belt about the waist. Little Chief was ready.

All this while Killer the Mandan stood with his weapons and his war horse watching the departing Sioux and waiting for Whirlwind. When he had armed his son, the Cheyenne chief came up to the Mandan and said, "Friend, stay in the camp. I go with my people who follow the Sioux. You are a brave man, but if you come with us there is sure to be trouble. Stay here. The Sioux may attack the camp. If they do not and you hear firing, come and fight with us."

Then Killer said, "*Ho!* I will do it." But his tongue was double.

Whirlwind turned from the Mandan to speak to

95

his wife. A-nu'tah sat in the lodge at her work. The sides of the tipi had been raised because of the heat, and the two men could see everything within it. The mother of the chief was singing softly to herself some war song of old times. She knew what was brewing, though she was old and blind.

The chief said to A-nu'tah, "I am going after the Sioux. Stay near the lodge and dig rifle pits. Do not be afraid. If the Sioux attack the camp, stay in the rifle pit and do not run around the camp like a crazy person. Keep quiet and lie low."

A-nu'tah sat in the tipi facing her husband, holding the moccasin unfinished in her hand. Beside her husband and a little behind him stood Killer. As the chief spoke to her, the Mandan spoke also, using the silent language of signs. No one could see the signs he was making to her, for he held his hands well down in front of his body, and the chief was busy with his own speech. A-nu'tah saw the signs that Killer made, but her face betrayed nothing to her husband. Killer said, "I am going to the big rock beyond the creek. Meet me there with a fast horse. Now is our time! You are my woman!"

Whirlwind jumped on his black war horse and rode away after the Sioux. Little Chief mounted his pony and followed his father, wearing the great warbonnet and the shield which his father had given him, feeling a warrior indeed. He had tasted the praise of the warriors when he killed the buffalo, and now he thirsted for the true glory of the fighting man. So he followed his father after the Sioux.

But Killer the Mandan jumped upon the pinto that Whirlwind had given him and rode away into the timber along the little creek as though he were going to scout round the camp, watching for the Sioux.

When all the men had gone, A-nu'tah took her best dress from the leather bag and put it on. She painted her face and took a decorated robe and went out of the lodge to choose a fast horse. All the best horses of the chief had been picketed about the lodge when the trouble began, to prevent the Sioux from stealing them. A-nu'tah knew that the fastest horse there was *Hochk*, the cream-colored race horse. She laid a robe on its back and on top of that a saddle of wood covered with rawhide, having a high pommel and a high cantle decorated with fringes and brass studs. She fastened bags of pemmican on the saddle and threw her robe over it. Then she mounted astride and rode quickly away into the timber.

When Whirlwind saw Little Chief following him out of camp he stopped and waited. When the boy overtook him he said, "My son, who will guard the camp if you go with me? Go back to the camp and keep watch. If the Sioux attack, bring word."

Little Chief turned back and rode slowly towards the camp, hanging his head. He was ashamed. "I am a man," he thought. "What shall I do in the camp? Let the boys and the old men guard the camp!" Little Chief was as near to tears as a warrior ever gets.

As the boy approached the camp he saw A-nu'tah mount his father's race horse and ride away into the timber. It was not fit that a woman should ride his father's race horse. Little Chief was angry. What was she doing, riding away like that after his father had told her to stay in the camp? Little Chief rode up to the tipi and questioned the old woman within. But she could tell him nothing, for she was blind. The boy quirted his pony and rode after A-nu'tah.

He crossed the dry bed of the creek, passed through the trees, and emerged in a shallow, grassy valley which led up from the water course. There he saw the Mandan and the woman together. They did not see him. They were busy, transferring the saddle to the gift horse. He stopped to watch, for he was frightened. What were they doing? It was not the custom for a man and a woman to meet outside the camp. While he watched, the pair changed mounts, so that Killer rode the race horse and A-nu'tah the gift horse.

Then the boy guessed what was being done. He was angry. He quirted his pony and rode after them. When they saw him coming, the woman would have run away, but the Mandan stopped and called to her to wait. He saw it was only a boy in warrior's clothing. Then she too recognized the boy. She was nervous and angry, and called to Killer, emphasizing her meaning with a gesture, "Kill him!" But the Mandan only laughed. He saw it was only a frightened boy.

Seeing them stop, Little Chief stopped too, for

he was very much afraid. Still the woman kept urging the Mandan to kill him. But Killer signaled, "Boy, go home! This is no place for you!" He had no ill will for Little Chief. The situation amused him. He laughed again.

When Little Chief knew what Killer meant and saw him laugh, he remembered what his father had said to him. He drew out his bow and began singing his war song. He had made a war song all his own, and the words of it went thus:

> *"There, as helpless I lay,*
> *Newborn, by my mother, then*
> *Did she not smile, did she not say—*
> *'Lo! I have borne a man?' "*

Often and often his grandmother had told him how his mother had rejoiced when he was born, though she died the same day. So the boy had made this song to remind him that he must play the man, keeping it secret even from his grandmother.

When he had finished singing the song, he gave the war whoop, quirted his pony and charged the Mandan, letting fly an arrow. But Killer swung sideways from the saddle as the arrow passed, and it missed him. And as Little Chief rode by, Killer thrust his lance into the boy so that it passed through his chest. Little Chief fell from the back of his pony, dragging the lance from the man's hand.

Then Killer left the lance in the body and took the woman and rode away quickly. But the boy's pony waited beside the body until the sun set and the wolves howled their evening chorus.

The Meeting of the Chiefs

CHAPTER VI

THE TWO BROTHER-FRIENDS

TRADITION has it that when the Cheyenes first ventured out of their native woods upon the great plains, they were suddenly attacked and badly beaten by a war party of another tribe. At that time the peaceful Cheyennes were almost unarmed and had had little experience of fighting. The beating they received made a profound impression upon them. After a time one of their old men arose and said, "We must learn to fight. We must fight everybody. Then we shall be great men." On this suggestion the tribe had acted ever since. They had indeed fought everybody. Few in number as compared with the tribes by which they were surrounded, they had made a place and a name for themselves, and had become indeed the great men of the prairies—fighters every one.

It was not in their sensitive, headstrong, high-spirited souls to endure insolence from any body of men. They had made concessions to the Sioux, and the Sioux had rejected them. Now all feeling of friendship and all restraint due to the laws of hospitality and the presence of the sacred calumets had vanished. The Cheyennes were furious, itching for occasion to fight. When they followed the retreating Sioux away from their women and children, the last motive for forbearance was removed. They craved vengeance, and numbers meant nothing to them.

They soon overtook the Sioux and mingled boldly with them, riding dauntlessly into the middle of the formation and pushing their ponies up to the most tumultuous and hot-headed warriors, with violent cries and fierce, insulting gestures. Their ponies shouldered the Sioux horses and brushed aside the trailing finery of their masters with an insolent deliberation of manner that contrasted strikingly with the threatening vociferations of the Cheyennes on their backs. The men of both parties burned with resentment.

The party rode slowly along, but both men and horses felt the restraint of inaction under such stress of emotion. The animals pranced, reared, and plunged in sympathy with the pent-up feeling of the men. Everywhere plumes were tossing and swaying, fists were shaken, weapons brandished, and men thrust their fierce faces, made perfectly demoniac by the war paint and the distortions of rage, into the faces of their adversaries. A single blow would have caused immediate battle and the loss of many lives.

Through all this tumult Ironshirt rode quietly along, saying very little, but alert and on his guard. He appeared quite unconcerned by the uproar and antics of the Cheyennes. But no one personally insulted him. He was ready to fight, if need be, but wished to avoid it because of the women and children ahead. In an impromptu battle some of these were sure to suffer. No man was braver in war, but Ironshirt was a father to his people, far-sighted, kind-hearted, and well beloved.

By his side rode Two Crows, his life-long comrade. When the two were mere boys they had hunted squirrels together with blunted arrows. Before they were grown they had formed one of those indissoluble unions, common among the Indians of the plains, which lasted throughout life and which can be compared only to the friendship of David and Jonathan. They had danced their first Sun Dance together; they were members of the same warrior order; in everything these two had worked and suffered together. Each had saved the life of the other in battle. Either would cheerfully have given his life for his friend.

As they rode along with apparent unconcern in the mob of howling savages, Two Crows remembered that Ironshirt had broken his medicine in the camp of the Cheyennes. His food had been touched by an iron spoon, and the charm which had protected him in battle was broken by that act. If a fight came on, Ironshirt would expose himself as usual, and the result would be certain death. A man could live only so long as the Mysterious Powers protected him. They had deserted Ironshirt. The ceremony of expiation which would restore the protective power of the coat of mail could not be performed where they were. It was long and tedious and required many things which were not at hand. A fight seemed certain to take place. Two Crows resolved to save Ironshirt from his fate. He rode up close to his comrade and said to him:

"Brother-friend, if the Cheyennes attack us, who will protect the women? They will be frightened and everyone will ride as fast as she can for home. They will be scattered all over the prairie and the Cheyennes will run them down and kill them. We cannot help it. But if you go to them you can keep them together and make them lie down and dig rifle pits. No one will be killed. The women will obey you. Take the old men and the boys and go to look after the women. I will stay here and form the warriors in line to hold back the Cheyennes."

He waited to see what Ironshirt would say.

Then Ironshirt turned to his comrade and replied, after a pause, "Brother-friend, what you say is true. I will go. I am no coward. But in the Cheyenne camp my food touched an iron spoon that was in the kettle. When I bought the iron shirt from the Kiowa, I was told not to eat such food. That broke my medicine. If I go into this fight I shall be killed. I know it."

The Sioux chief harangued his tribesmen, riding at a gallop through the formation. He showed no regard for the Cheyennes who stood in his path, but pushed them roughly aside with the shoulders of his horse with a composure equalled only by their excitement. At once the Sioux halted and formed in line. Ironshirt and Two Crows rode along the line, calling out certain men—mostly old men and mere boys—who moved forward a few paces and at the word of command followed their chief on the trail of the fleeing women. Two Crows formed the remaining warriors into line facing the Cheyenne camp, which lay behind the hills a mile or two away.

Meanwhile, Ironshirt and his followers had overtaken the women and halted them. Already some of the women had far outdistanced the others, and it took some time to bring these back to the spot selected by their chief. This was a broad, flat stretch of buffalo grass, thickly spotted with shallow buffalo wallows, whose bare, dish-like depressions, dried and baked by the sun, afforded some shelter to a man lying prone. Here the horses were bunched and unloaded. Around the animals the baggage was piled in a continuous line, forming a barricade about two feet high, which was speedily improved by the rifle pits which the women began to dig behind it. Ironshirt distributed his men about the

barricade and made the women and children lie
down where bullets would not be likely to find
them. His fortification had a wide field of fire and
lay at the top of a considerable rise, so that there
was no chance for the enemy to approach under
cover. The short, curly buffalo grass hugged the
ground so closely that even the tawny ground squirrels could find no concealment. The place was well
adapted for defense.

Ironshirt's chief concern was that the Cheyennes
might charge the barricade and frighten the horses
picketed or held in the middle of his little fortification. The Cheyennes had few guns, and he thought
he could keep them at a distance in a duel of rifle
fire. But if a successful charge were made and the
horses stampeded, a good many people might be
hurt and the Sioux left afoot in the midst of a hostile
country. For the present the horses were quiet
enough. They were mostly logy pack animals, and
there were few flies on the windswept hilltop to
bother them.

The warriors primed their guns and examined
the flints, ready to fire at a moment's warning. Some
of the old women began to sing wolf songs to en-
courage the men, crouching behind the baggage
and scraping away with their knives at the hard
upland soil.

When Two Crows formed the Sioux into line
facing the camp, the Cheyennes immediately withdrew and fell into line opposite them, at a distance
of about one hundred paces. They were still shout-

ing and gesticulating at the Sioux, who now answered in kind. Both parties were so worked up that some of the younger men actually foamed at the mouth. But nothing was done, as no one took the initiative in the attack.

Two Crows saw that the Cheyennes were in no mood to retreat. He made up his mind to frighten them home. He shouted instructions to his men, telling them that he was about to charge the Cheyenne line, and that, when they saw him strike the first enemy, they must follow him at a gallop. Then Two Crows rode out before his warriors and charged down the slope at the Cheyenne line. On his left arm he carried a white shield, and rode his little red war horse bareback, controlling it by a lariat lashed round its lower jaw. The other end of the lariat was tied to his waist, as was not unusual in battle. His body was naked save for moccasins and breechcloth, and painted all over with a bright yellow ochre. In his scalp-lock two eagle feathers stood upright. He was unarmed, and carried a bone-handled quirt in his right hand.

He charged straight up to the Cheyenne line, intending to strike the warrior at the end of it. In Indian warfare individual prowess counted for more than concerted effort. The exhibition of courage was a far greater success than the mere killing or scalping of an enemy. To count coup—that is, to strike an enemy with the hand or with a short stick or weapon held in the hand, was the honor most coveted by the warrior of the prairies. Such exploits gave a man prestige and were recounted at all important public gatherings, such as the Sun Dance. Often enough, prominent warriors went into battle armed only with a switch or a whip with which to strike the enemy, thus demonstrating their daring and increasing their reputation in the most effective manner.

Warriors were rated by the number and quality of their coups, and not at all, as so many have supposed, by the number of scalps they had taken. Not infrequently some laggard took the scalp, while the daring leader ran on after the enemy who still showed fight. Four men might count coup on a single enemy, and these four ranked on that occasion in the sequence of their blows. Whenever a warrior fell, there was a general rush on the part of his enemies to be the first to strike him, and only too often daring men lost their lives and sacrificed the victory of the main body in their eagerness to touch a wounded man. For a wounded man was often much more dangerous than the same man unhurt.

When Two Crows reached the Cheyenne line he swerved to the right and struck at the warrior there with his quirt. At the same instant the Cheyenne thrust at Two Crows with his lance. But the Cheyenne's horse was excited by the sudden onrush of the Sioux and by the quirt waved over its head. It jumped to one side, pushing against the horse next to it, and neither man touched the other.

The Sioux rode on at a gallop along the front of

the Cheyenne line, looking for an opportunity to strike, dodging behind his horse to avoid the random bullets of his enemies, and shouting taunts and insults at them. As he passed, the Cheyennes reached for him with their lances over the ponies' heads, but Two Crows rode just out of reach and approached the farther end of the line unhurt.

One of the Cheyennes there had urged his horse forward a few steps, so that he was well ahead of the formation. He had an arrow on his bowstring. Two Crows saw him waiting there, and made up his mind to strike the man. Before Two Crows could reach him, the Cheyenne loosed his arrow. The Sioux would have swung behind his horse to avoid the shaft, but it was too late. The arrow pierced his thigh, passing through and pinning him to his frightened horse.

When the pony felt the point in its side, it seemed to go crazy and ran wildly across the prairie, in spite of all that Two Crows could do. The Sioux line, which had begun to advance, now halted, while the Cheyennes began to shoot faster than before. The Sioux returned the fire, and the battle began.

The firing went on for some time, for neither side took the initiative of charging. At such long range their bullets were mostly wasted, and nothing was accomplished until Gray Thunder rushed up under cover of the smoke of the Sioux guns and shot arrows into them at close range. One of the Sioux was killed and fell from his horse. At once a number of Cheyennes rushed up to count coup on the fallen man, but the Sioux crowded around the body and prevented them from approaching it. There was a little skirmish, and then the Cheyennes rode back to their own line. When the breeze swept away the smoke from that part of the line, the Cheyennes could see the Sioux putting the dead man across his horse and taking him back to the barricade, but they made no attempt to interfere. The chiefs would not permit them to break up into small parties. The Sioux outnumbered them too much.

Two Crows could neither stop his horse nor disengage himself from it. The arrow had penetrated into the animal's flesh beyond the barb on the arrowhead. Struggle as he would, the horse resisted his efforts successfully, and ran round and round over the prairie like a wild thing. Finally, when it had winded itself, he managed to stop the pony near the barricade, where Ironshirt and his party waited, watching the battle.

Two or three ran out and held the horse while Ironshirt helped his friend dismount. The blood had softened the sinew which bound the head to the shaft of the arrow, and he was able to draw out the shaft from the side of the plunging pony, leaving the triangular arrowhead in the wound. After Two Crows had dismounted, Ironshirt drew the shaft carefully from his friend's thigh. The hurt seemed only a flesh wound, and Two Crows made light of it. He asked for another horse to return to the fight. But Ironshirt and the others persuaded him to rest for a while on a buffalo robe behind the barricade, while he told them what had happened.

While he was talking, the body of the warrior who had been killed was laid across his horse, brought back, and turned over to his family. The women began to cry and wail and gash themselves with knives. This excited the Sioux men and made them very restless. It was hard to hear the women wailing and weeping and to sit still doing nothing. Ironshirt's eyes burned, though his strong face gave no sign of his agitation, as he sat looking across the baggage at the fight.

From his hilltop he could see the Sioux silhouetted against the white smoke of their rifles, moving about here and there, but keeping their formation, and shooting in an irregular, desultory fashion at their enemies beyond. Much farther away on the slope of the opposite hillside and—from his position —above the Sioux, the line of mounted Cheyennes was plain to be seen. Individuals could not be distinguished at that distance. The line appeared to be solid and marked by three strata of different colors —motley at the bottom where the horses gave the color; dull red above that, where naked bodies showed above the ponies' heads; black at the top with tufts of white at intervals, where some warbonnet crested the dark line of glossy hair. They held their formation steadily. It was evident that the Cheyennes were in no mood to go home.

Ironshirt watched the fight anxiously. Both

parties held their ground and fired, but nothing was being accomplished, no decisive action that might settle the thing one way or another. What was needed was a charge that would break the enemy's line, scatter his forces, and make it possible for the Sioux to proceed with their march.

While they watched, they could see a Cheyenne riding back and forth in the open before his line, and shortly after a number of others rode out and joined him in a charge on the Sioux. The Sioux gave ground, and one of their young men fell. When the watchers at the barricade saw that, they all looked to their war chief sitting there behind the baggage, doing nothing to help his warriors who were being killed. The fallen man had been recognized, and the women of his kin began wailing and crying to the warriors in the barricade to take pity on them and avenge his death. Still Ironshirt sat quiet, watching the fight and saying nothing, his robe about his knees.

Then One Horn left his post in the rifle pits and came to his son and said, "My son, why are you here with the women? Your young men need you out there, and here you sit behind the pack saddles. Those young men are all yours. You are the leader of the Strong Hearts. But here you sit under cover while your friends are being killed!"

Ironshirt looked round at the faces of his comrades and laughed grimly. Then he said, "Father, what you say is true. Stay here, all of you, and guard the women. I am going to avenge my friends."

Two Crows stood up and said, "Brother-friend, do not go. They will surely kill you!"

But Ironshirt made no reply. He took his lance, mounted his white war horse, and rode away to the fight.

When the Sioux saw their chief coming, they were encouraged and drove back the Cheyennes who had charged them. They had lost two men, but the presence of their invincible war chief inspirited them. They belonged to him and would follow him anywhere.

As Ironshirt came out from behind the line of Sioux, galloping towards the Cheyennes, he was singing a war song of the Strong Hearts. The words of the song referred to the qualifications of the Order, which admitted only men of proved courage, generosity, and worth:

> *"Friends, the man who runs away cannot be admitted!"*

Singing this song, he charged the Cheyennes.

When the Cheyennes saw the famous chief coming, they were uneasy. He was wearing the iron shirt above a shirt of soft buckskin. There was nothing to conceal the coat of mail, and they could all see it. It reached from his neck to his knees, and the sleeves extended to the elbows. The fine links of the Spanish mail were unbroken, and covered him effectively against the points of arrows, lances, or knives. He had only to fear bullets at close range. But the Cheyennes were afraid of the mysterious

115

protective power believed to reside in the shirt. Metal of any sort was a little uncanny to their Stone Age minds. They knew that this shirt had always protected the chief in battle. He had never been wounded. What could a man do against a champion covered by invulnerable armor?

Therefore, when Ironshirt came charging towards them, their line gave ground a little. He turned and swept along their line, singing his song and keeping his horse close to the heads of the Cheyenne ponies. As he advanced, the warriors reined in their ponies and gave back a little, as soldiers move back when dressing their lines. He dashed along their front swift as an arrow, shouting taunts and urging them to shoot at him, the invulnerable, in sheer bravado. He turned back to his own line unhurt.

Passing along the front of the Sioux, he turned and once more charged the Cheyennes, sweeping along their front as before, but rather nearer, for he was determined to intimidate them and make them run. The Cheyennes gave ground again, and some rather hastily pulled back their ponies long before Ironshirt arrived in their neighborhood. The man's confidence unnerved them.

The third time Ironshirt charged the Cheyennes, brandishing the lance-banner of the Strong Hearts and singing his song, the line gave way and began to break up into little groups, but some of the older warriors called out and the line just held. The Cheyennes began to shoot at the Sioux chief, though they had little hopes of hurting him. They were getting nervous. They knew the power of the iron shirt, and they were afraid of the Sioux chief and his song.

The fourth time Ironshirt charged the Cheyenne line, he felt that he would succeed in driving them away. They had fired at him, but he had taken no harm. His confidence and courage began to rise. He sang louder than ever, and he knew that the Sioux line waited for the first sign of the breaking up of the Cheyenne formation to follow him at a run and turn their near defeat into overwhelming victory. Already the Sioux, anticipating the result, came on at a walk behind him. He poised his lance and charged.

The Cheyennes did not wait for him. Heretofore, they had been startled by his sudden and harmless rushes, as a man walking on the prairie at evening is startled and quickens his pace when the harmless bull-bat swoops roaring at his head, only to return in erratic flight to the pursuit of the gnats on which she feeds. But now they broke and ran as young quail scatter and seek cover under the shadow of the hawk. Their ponies swung round in their tracks and ran for it before the Sioux chief had crossed half the wide stretch of yellow buffalo grass that lay between the lines.

The Charge

At this moment, Whirlwind, the Cheyenne chief, came galloping up from the rear. He had been de-

The Charge

layed by the arming of his son, and had been coming as fast as possible since he heard the first shot
fired. Just as he came up the Cheyenne line broke
into a dozen groups and ran back towards him,
while the Sioux gave a great shout and started in
pursuit. As Whirlwind watched, the Sioux swept
down the slope.

It was a magnificent sight—the long irregular line
of running ponies, their riders aflutter with feathers
and flowing hair, shaking their weapons and shouting the war whoop, obscured here and there by
little puffs of white smoke where some one fired at
the retreating Cheyennes. Well in advance rode
Ironshirt, holding on high the feathered lance-banner of his Order, his warbonnet streaming in the
wind, confident and victorious, the war cry uttered
by three hundred throats echoing in his ears.

As his flying tribesmen passed him, Whirlwind
stopped his horse, and began shouting to them to
stop and fight, not to run away like women. Some
of them heard him and attempted to pull up their
ponies. Others gave no heed, but flashed past, quirting their ponies as hard as they could. Those who
stopped began calling to the others to come back.

Whirlwind jumped off his horse, and turning the
animal loose, gave it a blow on the rump with his
bow that sent it running after the other Cheyenne
ponies, dragging the lariat by its side.

The chief wore the long leather sash of a leader
of the Dog Soldiers. It passed over his right shoulder and trailed on the ground at his feet. He took

his lance and thrust the point through the free end of this sash deep into ground, thus staking himself to his post of duty. It was the obligation of the leaders of this Order never to run away from a fight when their comrades retreated, but to stake themselves to the ground, and die, if need be, rather than budge from the spot. They were forbidden to pull up their lances, once planted. Only a comrade could do that for them.

Whirlwind wore the full costume or uniform of his Order. His face and body were anointed with sacred red paint. On his head was a cap thickly tufted with the feathers of the crow and the hawk, standing erect all over the crown and dominated by a lofty crest of eagle plumes bearing tassels of horsehair. His sash was richly worked with porcupine quills and decorated with feathers. On a thong about his neck hung a whistle made of the wing bone of an eagle. His long hair, wavy from its recent plaiting, flowed freely over his shoulders and down his back, concealing there the belt of black and white skunk skins which supported the breechcloth of red strouding which reached to his knees. His leggings were of white buckskin marked with many transverse black lines recording his exploits, and adorned with a heavy beaded strip and thick fringes of human hair along the seams. On his moccasins was embroidered the morning star, and from either ankle a skunk skin dragged the ground. In his right hand he held a rattle shaped like a snake and covered with clicking antelope hoofs. In his left hand he carried a sinew-backed bow and four sharp arrows. He had no other arms.

Having planted his lance, Whirlwind faced the enemy and began shaking his rattle and blowing the bone whistle, which emitted a sound not unlike the scream of an eagle. When the Cheyennes saw their chief dismount and drive away his horse and heard the whistle, they began to come back and reform their line. The Sioux, seeing this, also slowed down before they reached Whirlwind. They would leave this daring man to be disposed of by their chief.

Ironshirt saw the Cheyennes coming back, and a glance over his shoulder showed him that the Sioux were halting. The bold stand of the Cheyenne chief had altered matters. The victory was yet to be won, and it would be won by the side whose champion triumphed in single combat to the death. Both parties would sit looking on, ready to pursue or fly as circumstances might dictate. The Plains Indians fought like wolves, alternately running and pursuing, as their enemies charged or fled. But where the chiefs met in single combat, the issue was never doubtful. Victory rested always with the party whose champion conquered. Ironshirt knew that the event lay with him. The fate of his people was in his hands.

He knew that the protective power of his coat of mail had been lost. The Mysterious Powers had deserted him. His time had come. He would be killed in this battle. But he would not draw back. Perhaps he might kill Whirlwind before he died.

Boldly he charged the lone man in the open, lying flat on his horse to avoid the arrows of his foe, and holding the lance in his right hand along the pony's neck at the height of a man's chest.

When Whirlwind saw the white stallion with the red crescent painted across its chest bearing down upon him at the gallop, he threw down the rattle he was shaking and dropped the eagle-bone whistle from his lips. He stood close to his upright lance, so that the tether would interfere as little as possible with his freedom of action. He knew the reputed power of the iron shirt. But he trusted in his own medicine and in the power of the Dog Soldiers. If the iron shirt had too great power, he knew he must die. If it had not this power, the victory would be his own.

As Ironshirt approached, Whirlwind quickly shot his four arrows. The first passed harmlessly through the feathers of the Sioux Chief's warbonnet. The second lodged in the face of the shield upon his back. The third and fourth struck the coat of mail and glanced off. The Cheyenne had only four arrows and stood defenseless, awaiting the charge. He was a brave man.

Ironshirt rode up on Whirlwind's right, intending to run him through with the lance. Seeing what was coming, the Cheyenne had shifted his hand to the end of his bow, and as the Sioux rushed up, struck the horse heavily across the face with the weapon. The animal reared high in the air, and shied away to avoid a second blow. The lance was turned aside. Ironshirt rode, as usual, without saddle or bridle. As the frantic horse swung round, Whirlwind seized the lance above the point, and with a sudden wrench, dragged it from the hand of his enemy. The sudden lurch of the pony, combined with the unexpected drag at the lance, unseated the Sioux, superb horseman though he was. He fell to the ground and rolled in the dust, while the animal ran away out of the field.

Whirlwind instantly reversed the lance and thrust at the Sioux, but Ironshirt sprang up out of his reach, hung his shield on his left arm, and drew his knife from its sheath—a broad, two-edged steel blade, hafted with the jaw bone of a bear on which the teeth and hair still remained, making an excellent grip, at once uneven and smooth. Raising this weapon, the Sioux rushed in on Whirlwind, and got safely past the point of the lance, which slipped harmlessly off his iron shirt. The Cheyenne dropped the lance, and cracked the knuckles of his foe with the bow, knocking the knife from his hand. It fell upon the ground, and both men scrambled for it, but the Sioux got it, for the sash hindered Whirlwind. Ironshirt came on again and struck the breast of his enemy. The blade glanced off the ribs, inflicting a slight wound. Whirlwind seized the knife-hand of the Sioux and the two men wrestled and struggled for the weapon.

Of the two, Whirlwind was the heavier, but was hampered by the sash dragging at his shoulders. Ironshirt was expecting his death, and fought with the fury of despair. He had the advantage of a close grip on the knife and nothing the other could do would break it. Three times Whirlwind succeeded in gaining a grip on the haft below the hand of his adversary, but each time the Sioux wrenched the blade away through his clinging fingers, cutting them severely and slicing deep into the palm of the hand. At such times the Sioux struck savagely at the body of his enemy, and inflicted a number of wounds in his breast and sides. But always Whirlwind grasped the knife again with bleeding fingers, and no serious harm was done him.

The men panted and sweat and struggled together, spattered with blood from the Cheyenne's wounds, but neither of them could get possession of the knife long enough to use it effectively. At length the Cheyenne's weight began to tell. He twisted and wrenched at the ivory haft, now slippery with blood, and when he felt the Sioux's fingers yielding, suddenly tripped him and jerked the knife from his hand as he fell. Before the unlucky man could roll out of the way, Whirlwind had raised the knife above him ready to strike.

Ironshirt sprang up and tried to escape the blow, but the Cheyenne caught the fleeing man by a long hair ornament of metal disks which hung at the back of his head, dragged him backwards to his knees and stabbed him again and again in the side of the neck until he collapsed on the trampled buffalo grass. A moment later, and Whirlwind held up to view the knife and the scalp of his enemy. Iron-shirt had met his fate.

At once the Cheyennes set up a great shout and charged at full speed, every man trying to be the first to touch the fallen chief. For a short time the disheartened Sioux warriors did nothing. Then, following the example of their leaders, they too charged, to rescue the body of their dead chief. Though the Cheyennes got a good start, the Sioux were much nearer, and arrived well in advance. As they came on, those on fast horses outstripped the others, and reached the spot some seconds before the rest.

In his struggle with Ironshirt, Whirlwind's sash had been torn loose from the lance, which still stood upright in the ground beside the dead body. The Cheyenne chief was freed. He might have evaded the charging Sioux. Instead, he stood waiting for them, shaking the knife he had taken from his enemy, and singing the war song of his Order:

> *"Oh Sun, thou endurest forever,*
> *But we Dog Soldiers must die!"*

The first warrior who came up tried to shoot the Cheyenne chief from behind his horse. But Whirl-wind ran up to him and dragged the gun from his hands as he fired it, then struck him down with the butt. The second carried a lance. As he rode up, Whirlwind stepped aside and avoided the point, then caught at the man's belt as the horse ran by, and swung himself up behind. Riding there, he threw one arm around his helpless adversary, and stabbed the unlucky Sioux in the side with his knife time after time, until the man tumbled to the ground.

The Cheyenne chief was now mounted. He turned the horse to face the main body of the Sioux, who were just coming up. He caught up his lance, which had remained standing in the ground, and charged them at top speed. He was a fearful spectacle, smeared with dust and blood, the knife in his teeth, and his long dishevelled hair flying about his face. As he came on, brandishing his lance, his long sash trailing backwards over his horse's haunches, with the Cheyenne warriors at his heels, the Sioux began to rein in their ponies. The leaders stopped, then turned, and the whole body scattered and raced for their lives, as boys going swimming scatter and scramble up trees when some old buffalo bull, fierce and lusty with his summer's feeding, comes charging out of a thicket, trailing vines and branches from his mighty horns, stamping and bellowing with rage.

The Cheyennes chased them, cutting off those who fell behind, capturing horses and weapons, counting coup freely upon the fallen and the flying, or stopping to strip and scalp the dead. Here and there a horse went down, and the rider was caught and killed. Elsewhere, some one made a daring rescue of a man left afoot and carried him off under the noses of the Cheyennes, the two Sioux riding double. At intervals, little groups paused for a short time to stand off the Cheyennes, while a fallen man was carried back to the barricade, then rode on as before.

It was only a short distance to the barricade—less than half a mile. Otherwise the fight might have been much more disastrous. But the Sioux were so numerous and the distance so short that they had no chance to become very widely scattered. And the Cheyennes, eager as they were for revenge, could not resist stopping in their pursuit to count coup or strip the fallen. So that, all things considered, the Sioux lost very few men.

They reached the barricade and took their stand behind it. When the Cheyennes attempted to advance, the firing became so heavy that smoke almost entirely blotted out the piled-up baggage behind which their enemies fought. Gray Thunder attempted a charge, but the Sioux fire was too hot to face, and the Cheyennes could not get near enough to use their arrows effectively. There was no cover behind which they might creep up unobserved, for the hilltop occupied by the Sioux was as smooth and bare as a horse's croup. The Sioux had lost the skirmish and some lives, but they were perfectly safe behind their barricade, and the Cheyennes could do nothing but fire at long range at a large but indefinite target. And Indian guns, often exposed to the weather as they were, rarely cleaned, never properly oiled, and usually of inferior workmanship to begin with, were not very deadly at long range in the hands of men who used them only in battle and never wasted priceless ammunition in practice shooting. Besides, not many of the Cheyennes had guns.

It was now late in the afternoon, and the Cheyennes disposed themselves about the Sioux barricade out of range, like wolves on the outskirts of a herd of buffalo. A few found shelter in buffalo wallows, where the fringe of tall grass about the rim of the depressions gave them a little cover from which to fire occasional bullets which might just reach their enemy. Others sat and smoked in circles on the grass, holding the lariats of their horses, or stalked about in their white robes, walking the sweating ponies. Here and there some daring young man rode back and forth within range, taunting the Sioux and trying to get them to come out and fight in the open. But Chief Two Crows, who had succeeded to the command, would not permit that.

Meanwhile, Whirlwind sat with the other chiefs, smoking calmly as though nothing had happened, and planning some way of making the Sioux come out and get into a running fight once more. The chiefs sent certain young men back to the camp for food and water, and when these returned about sunset, little cooking fires were lighted here and there just out of range, and the hungry Cheyennes ate supper. They enjoyed this the more because they knew that the Sioux had no water and must be very thirsty.

When it became dark, the young men began to talk of creeping up on the Sioux near enough to use their arrows. The night was dark and cloudy, and a number made the attempt successfully, and came back telling of the sounds they had heard after shooting into the dark mass within the barricade. But Two Crows threw out scouts around his fortification who soon put an end to this enterprise, so that nothing useful was accomplished.

All night the mules within the barricade made a hideous uproar, bawling and squealing like the vicious brutes they were, preventing all sleep. The Cheyennes could hear, too, the wailing and crying of the women of the dead Sioux. There was singing and shouting back and forth at intervals all night. Fortunately for the Sioux, huddled together as they were among their horses in the cramped fortification, there were very few mosquitoes on the windswept hilltop to annoy the animals and make them restless.

During the night the Cheyennes planned that with the first gray dawn they would try to stampede the horses of the Sioux. They believed that it would be easy to do this by getting near the barricade before it was light enough to use guns effectively. Accordingly, when the darkness that precedes the dawn smothered the starlight on the prairie, the young men selected for this exploit quietly mounted and cautiously advanced. Their horses had all been chosen because of their dark color, and the Sioux did not see them coming until after they heard the tread of the ponies' feet. The young men were spread out in a long line with wide intervals between, and when the Sioux discovered them, they thought the Cheyennes were making a charge. At once the night was punctuated with sharp flashes of fire and whirling puffs of white smoke. The Cheyennes rushed the barricade at full speed, shooting their guns in the air, waving their robes round their heads, and shouting as loud as they could to frighten the horses.

The Sioux crowded to the barrier to repel the charge, and many of the horses were left untended. They threw up their heads, startled by the sudden uproar, then began to stir uneasily among the people in the barricade. Some of the Sioux sprang out of the rifle pits to hold the horses, but a Cheyenne arrow struck one of the mules in the flank and he bolted, squealing and knocking over several people as he blundered through the piled-up baggage.

The white hide of this animal attracted others, and as the howling line of Cheyennes swept past the barricade, yelping and waving their buffalo robes, half-hidden by the swirling smoke of the Sioux rifles, most of the horses broke away and ran wildly out into the open as hard as they could go. Here and there a horse went down when he stepped upon the trailing lariat of another and lost his footing in the mad scramble. Several were badly scarred by the picket pins which whirled and bounded in dangerous arcs at the ends of the ropes, dealing ugly blows in the darkness.

The main body of the Cheyennes had formed in line behind the young men who were to stampede the herd. These now charged at the gallop up the slope towards the barricade in the wake of the others. Some of the Sioux women had been hurt and knocked down by the stampeding horses, and their crying mingled with the sounds of shooting and confusion in the fortification as the charge suddenly swept down upon them. Two Crows heard the Cheyennes coming and rallied his men to the barricade. When Whirlwind and his warriors arrived, the Sioux were ready, and gave them such a warm reception that the charge was split and swept by on either side the entrenchment without much damage to anybody. Before the Cheyennes could get together again and re-form for another charge, it had become so light that it was thought best not to attempt it.

Instead, the Cheyennes occupied themselves in rounding up and catching the horses of the Sioux, which were running in every direction over the prairie. Every man could claim as his own the animals he caught, and there was an exciting half hour spent in the scramble to get as many as possible.

The feelings of the Sioux in their dry camp on the hilltop may be imagined as each one watched some Cheyenne take possession of his favorite war horse and ride away. They were powerless to interfere, for even had they wished to make a charge and recover their mounts, they had only a few old sore-backed pack horses to ride, and the Cheyennes would simply have run away and laughed at them for their pains. It was fortunate for the Sioux that their home camp was so near. For of all misfortunes to try a man's soul, none could exceed that of being left afoot in the midst of the plains.

It was now broad day, and the Cheyennes took council over their food. It was obvious that nothing further could be accomplished by charging the Sioux. They had beaten them in open fight, had taken two-thirds of their best horses, and with this —and the scalps they had taken—the Cheyennes were content. In the afternoon they left scouts to watch the Sioux and rode away in little groups towards home, having agreed to meet at the big rock outside the entrance to the camp to prepare for the triumphal march into the village.

Arrived there, the warriors washed off the dust of battle, anointed their faces and bodies with the black paint of victory, arranged their war costumes to the best advantage, and made ready to mount. The scalps they had taken were seven in number. These they had cleaned and stretched upon small hoops a few inches in diameter, which they now attached to the tops of slender, peeled willow wands. When all were ready, the men mounted and formed in a long line opposite the entrance to the village, but quite out of sight from it. The trees along the creek screened them from the camp. It was usual to charge on the camp when a war party returned from a successful expedition, and this spectacular entrance was now about to take place. Those who had taken scalps carried the wands to which they were fastened upright in the air, while others held in their hands captured guns and other trophies of the battle.

Whirlwind, as the principal hero of the occasion, was selected to ride on the extreme right end of the line of warriors. He was mounted upon Ironshirt's white stallion, having turned his own horse loose on approaching the camp. He carried the feathered lance-banner which he had taken from the Sioux and to which he had fastened his scalp. The coat of mail had been entirely destroyed by the Cheyennes, who were afraid of it, as they did not know the regulations and tabus which belonged to it.

When all were ready and the line formed at the

top of the little grassy valley which led down to the stream by the camp, Whirlwind placed his eagle-bone whistle at his lips and blew shrilly the signal to advance, brandishing his lance and setting his own horse in motion. At once the whole line plunged forward in a race for the camp circle, the warriors whooping and yelling and firing their guns as they rode, leaping their horses over stones and bushes, while the thin strands of hair at the tops of the willow wands danced and jumped merrily above their heads. The triumphal entry had begun.

CHAPTER VII

THE WELCOME OF THE WARRIORS

THOSE Cheyennes who had remained in camp—mostly old men, women, and children—had learned the details of the fighting from the young men who had come into camp the day before to get food and water for the war party, and they were not taken unawares when they heard the first exultant whoop of the returning warriors. All had put on their best clothes and anointed their faces with black paint in honor of the victory. When the line of shouting horsemen in all their warlike finery broke upon the camp like a flood, driving the captured horses before it, pouring between the tipis through clouds of rifle smoke and golden sunset dust, and, with the

Sioux scalps tossing above their heads, swept to the very center of the camp circle in a whirlwind of triumph, the stay-at-homes stood by their tipi doors and greeted their heroes with singing and shrill cries.

After the charge the warriors formed in column of fours for their parade. Then it was noticed that Whirlwind, who had been selected by the chiefs to ride with Gray Thunder some distance in advance of the column as a mark of especial bravery, was absent. This caused a short delay, but the enthusiasm ran too high to permit anything to hinder the festivities long, and the chiefs named another man to ride with Gray Thunder. Starting at the entrance of the camp, the long column paraded around at a walk inside the great circle of tipis, and then, reversing its direction, marched round the camp outside. As they rode proudly along, the warriors waved their trophies and chanted the age-old exultant Song of the Victors:

"We have hair!"

and another favorite, celebrating their success in stampeding the Sioux ponies:

"Sister, I bring you his horses!"

It was a time of triumph indeed, and a stirring spectacle, as the column moved steadily round the circle through the calm, clear air of evening, under the burnished clouds of the sunset.

That was a great sight. Other troops of mounted

men have been splendidly mounted and handsomely equipped. But what other headdress is so noble and gorgeously swagger as the warbonnet, which sways and flutters with the lightest breeze or movement of its wearer? What uniform can compare with the lithe, athletic grace of the nude warrior? What stable-bred mount can rival, in such a pageant, the half-wild war horse of the plains? What music is at once so weirdly barbaric and so appealing to the cosmic instincts? What war cry is so terribly expressive of the blood-lust and the triumph of man overcoming his kind? If war is primitive, it requires a primitive setting, primitive actors. The modern world can show nothing to compare with this, and this it will see no more.

A number of Arapaho visitors in the camp had watched the Cheyennes ride off to battle, but had remained quietly in their tipis during the trouble with the Sioux, taking no part in the fighting. Now, as neither they nor their kin had had any share in the victory, the Arapahos still wore the red face-paint of an Indian at peace. And so, when, among the throng of blackened faces, the Cheyenne warriors noticed their red cheeks, and remembered that these Arapahos, their allies, had let them ride off to fight against great odds without offering to join the party, the whole column suddenly struck up the taunting melody of the old Song of Reproach:

> *"What men are these with reddened faces?*
> *What brave men took their places?*

We rode to the fight
In broad daylight."

As the column of warriors passed along the curving line of tipis, it was cheered with all the enthusiasm which a complete victory over superior numbers always aroused. Old men with shriveled shanks and watery eyes stood trembling with excitement, tapping their polished staves on the ground in time to the music, and chanting the familiar songs in a shrill, throaty quaver; children stood entranced and half-frightened by the stern faces and swaying plumes of the warriors and clinging fast to their mothers' skirts; old women, bold with the privilege of years and matronhood, chanted loudly with the men or gave shrill war cries, fiercer than their own; while the shy girl, her painted face and beautifully beaded garments half-concealed under the robe shared with a chum, gestured vivaciously with slender, braceleted wrists, listening to the subdued chatter of her companions and covertly watching for the haughty face of some young man.

The old mother of Whirlwind stood beside the painted tipi, singing and shouting with enthusiasm, as the warriors passed. She knew that her son had distinguished himself, and her blind old eyes could not see that Whirlwind was not with the others. But the wives of the chief were uneasy at his absence, and when the formation broke up, made anxious inquiry about him. But no one could tell them anything, except that he had started in the charge with the others.

When the warriors charged the camp, Whirlwind was riding on the extreme right. As they advanced pell-mell over the uneven ground, studded with rocks and bushes, the chief found his path rapidly shelving away into a crumbling cut-bank, washed out by some spring freshet. He turned his horse to the right to find better footing, and so became separated by several yards from the others, who gained upon him because of his change in direction. However, they were still in plain view, and he knew that, once across the stream and in the open, his white horse could show its heels to them all.

As he rode on at full speed, a small clump of bushes rose in his path. He set his mount to the leap to avoid going round. The horse cleared the obstacle—then, in mid air, suddenly jerked convulsively, trying to extend its leap to avoid something which lay beneath it on the grass. Whirlwind was almost unseated, and as the horse came down, saw at a glance what had caused the animal's fright— some fallen Sioux, his ribs picked clean by the wolves, thrust through with a lance.

As soon as he could master his mount, Whirlwind turned back towards the skeleton to count the coup. As he did so, he recognized the lance of Killer the Mandan, and smiled to think how good a defender of the camp his guest had been. It was unlikely that any other warrior had seen the body, and the chief made haste to it to strike the blow, intending to follow the warriors into the camp and take part in the procession immediately after. He would have honor enough later, and even these bones were worth the striking. The skeleton, somewhat disarranged by the wolves, lay clean and white on the trampled grass, as Whirlwind rode up with ready lance. But the blow was never struck.

The heart of the chief suddenly stopped, swelled, and hung numb within his breast. Bones he had seen in plenty, and death was his trade and sport. But beside that slender skeleton lay the dragon-fly shield and decorated quiver of his boy. And still attached to the skull and mingling with the long black hair, lay the bedraggled eagle feathers and ermines of the warbonnet which he had himself so often worn. It was his son . . . his *son!* And the Mandan's lance . . . The shield had failed his son! *His medicine had failed!* He felt helpless and frightened. His *medicine* had failed his son!

Whirlwind swore no vow of vengeance. That was
to be taken for granted. And a glance at the stale
"sign" about told him that, with such a start as the
Mandan had, it was useless to pursue. Indeed, he
was scarcely conscious of the thought. He was too
dull, too numb to think of such matters . . . his son
. . . his son . . . his all . . . his pride and hope . . . *Ki'as!*
He could not realize it. For a long time he stood
motionless, staring at what lay on the grass. Then
he got slowly on his horse, like an old man, and rode
at a walk through the gathering dusk towards the
camp.

When he dismounted at his tipi, his wives came
running up with cries of satisfaction, but he appeared not to notice them. They saw that something
had gone wrong, and made an end of their demon-
strations. But his old mother could not see. She was
singing a song in his praise when he rode up, and as
he approached the tipi, she ran out and caught hold
of him and hugged him hard with all the force of
her energetic affection, passing her hands over his
face and taking on over him as mothers will. He
still carried in his hand the feathered lance-banner
captured from Ironshirt, with the scalp attached.
This the old woman snatched from him. She hobbled away, holding to the hand of her little grand-
daughter, talking volubly as she went, breaking into
shrill cries of triumph and singing old victory songs,
to join the women of other successful warriors in the
middle of the camp.

She found almost the whole population of the

camp gathered there about a huge pile of dry logs which had just been set on fire. As she came up, the crier was calling the last of the people to come and take part in the dance. Everyone was in gala attire. The men wore full war costume. Some carried the weapons and wore the regalia of the warrior order to which they belonged. Others wore costumes of which they had dreamed. All took care to display the tokens of their prowess in battle. All were wrapped in buffalo robes crossed by a broad strip of beads or quill-work relieved at intervals by large rosettes. Some of these robes had lively pictures of the exploits of their wearers, showing a profusion of horses, warriors, guns, pony tracks, and other hieroglyphics in red and black.

The women were fully as carefully dressed as the men. The victory dance was one of those social functions—not very frequent in savage life—at which women had an opportunity to display their charms before the young men. They naturally took advantage of it. Painted buffalo robes, elaborately embroidered leggings, moccasins, and smocks with long soft fringes and scalloped edges made bright with vermilion; rings and bracelets of steel and silver; earrings and pendants; jet-black hair, parted in the middle from forehead to nape, terminating in two glossy braids; such was their costume. Their faces were shining with paint and good humor as they sat in groups on the grass waiting for the dance to begin.

A group of men gathered near the fire began

humming and tapping gently upon the small drums which they held in their hands. As they found the pitch and gained confidence, this drumming began to sound louder and louder, until at last it was in full swing, regular, steady and firm as the pulse, with a cosmic rhythm that called to the blood of the victorious Cheyennes.

At the command of the crier, the women fell into line facing the fire, carrying in their hands the willow wands to which the scalps were attached, and other trophies of the battle given them by their kinsmen. On the other side of the fire the men formed in a like manner. The two arcs joining, a circle was formed, and as the drums struck up again, this moved round and round, always to the left, the dancers standing shoulder to shoulder, and singing as they moved. The step was very simple. The left knee was held stiff, and the right was suddenly bent at every step with a sidewise, swaying motion much more vigorous than the short distance covered warranted. Thus the whole circle, wedged together, swayed as a unit to the music as it advanced.

The circle was very large, as almost all the men of the camp had taken part in the fight, and they and all their women engaged in dancing. Within the circle the drummers, twenty or more in number, marched contrary to the dancers, round and round and to and from the fire, singing and beating their small hand drums with padded sticks. Here and there in the circle single figures danced with a different step, bending and leaping and brandishing their weapons, boasting of their exploits in the battle.

Then the step became more lively, the scalps and captured weapons were waved on high, and the song rose and fell with more volume as the women's shrill voices were added to the deep bass of the men's. The dancers within the circle imitated the actions of the fight, shrill war cries sounded above the din, and for a moment a perfect vertigo of enthusiasm was indulged. Then the music dropped again to the previous rhythm, and the dance continued as before. Here and there some young man stepped into the line of women, and enveloping the girl of his choice within the folds of his own robe, danced on around, talking to her and caressing her. The buffalo robe was the only shelter in which young people could make love in a Cheyenne camp, but it screened them from the public gaze effectively enough, even in the midst of such an uproar as this.

Meanwhile the older men and the chiefs sat smoking near the fire, gravely discussing the probability of an attack by the Sioux after the latter had reached home with their women and got fresh mounts. It was not likely that the Sioux would be so cowed as not to retaliate. And the Cheyennes were ready to move south for the winter hunt, anyway. They waited only to loot the baggage which the Sioux must leave behind them.

Of all those exultant people, the mother of Whirl-

wind was most delighted. Her own life was dull
enough. She lived only in her son, and his triumphs
were her greatest pleasures. As the dance went on,
her vigor and enthusiasm were not abated, in spite
of her seventy winters. She sang and hobbled, hobbled and sang, shaking the lance and scalp of Ironshirt, giving the war whoop, and arousing a deal of
sympathetic merriment by her hearty joy. Though
the dance continued till morning, folk said, the old
blind woman would be there still, displaying more
energy and enthusiasm than any other. She was a
woman of character and a leader of her sex, and of
all things she loved the Scalp Dance most.

When Whirlwind entered his tipi, one of his
wives spread a robe for him to sit upon and brought
water to wash his hands. The other brought food in
a wooden bowl and a pair of fresh moccasins to
replace the worn and blood-stained ones he had
worn in the battle. But the chief wanted none of
these things. He told the women to harness a pack
horse and go with him. The women, sensing that
something was wrong, but not daring to ask what,
made haste to obey. They caught an old pack horse,
placed the travois on its back, and in a few moments moved off. One of the women led the horse,
the other followed behind. Whirlwind walked in
advance.

The women knew that A-nu'tah was missing
since noon the day before, and thought that their
husband's mood had something to do with this. But

they judged silence best, and followed him without a word.

When the silent party reached the spot where Little Chief had fallen, the women were very much frightened. It was dark, and they were afraid of the dead. And when they realized that it was Little Chief who lay there, gruesome and white in the gloom, the overwrought creatures began to wail and cry and tear their clothing, after the custom of mourners. But the chief soon put an end to that, brusquely telling them to be quiet and do as he told them. He was so terrible in his steady silence, that the women smothered their grief and controlled themselves, save for an occasional sob. Whirlwind placed his son's bones on his buffalo robe spread flat on the grass. Then the women folded the robe over the skeleton and laced it with thongs into a long bundle. The bundle they laid upon the travois, lashing it there securely with a lariat. Then the little party moved towards camp, one of the women watching the load while the other led the horse. Whirlwind walked behind carrying the warbonnet and shield of his son on one arm and the lance of Killer the Mandan in his hand.

When they reached the tipi, it was quite dark, and Whirlwind bade the women clear out the lodge and build up a fire. They made haste to do so, and soon there was only the couch of the chief remaining in the painted tipi. This bed was made of willow rods as thick as the little finger, straightened and tied into a mat with sinew cords. At either end the mat was raised against a tripod of cedar poles, so that a man could recline against it in comfort. The raised portions of the mat were gaily painted and decorated with tassels of clicking deer's hoofs. On this bed the chief made the women spread a buffalo robe, with soft cushions of deerskin, stuffed with buffalo wool, and embroidered with varicolored lines of bead-work and tufts of red wool. Behind this bed he had hung up a new canopy of whitened cowskin, adorned in a similar manner, very clean and pretty. On the mat at the head of the bed he fastened the skin of the calf that Little Chief had killed, suspended by the nose, and above that the shield, quiver, and warbonnet in its rawhide case, with the bags of paints and medicine. Over the bed he hung up the Mandan's lance. Then, when all things were ready, he told the women to lay his son on the couch.

Trembling, they carried out all his instructions in haste and hurried out of the lodge, where the flickering fire cast ghostly shadows round the gray walls. But Whirlwind called them back and told them to bring food for his son, who was weary. Then one of them brought dried meat in a bowl, laid it beside the body on the couch, and ran out of the lodge.

The terrified women told others of the strange actions of Whirlwind, and before long the story had got about the camp. Some bold ones approached the tipi, and looking in through rents in the hides, went away vouching for the truth of the story,

which came, at length, to the ears of Whirlwind's mother.

When the old woman heard that Little Chief was dead and her son gone mad, she scoffed at the tale and continued the dance. Often before, her blindness had tempted people to hoax her, and she was not to be fooled so easily. But when an old crony came to her and reproached her publicly for dancing when there was death in the lodge, she made haste to hobble back to the darkened tipi where Whirlwind sat with his son.

There the other women informed her in terrified whispers of what had taken place, and the old woman, now no longer able to deny the truth of the story, tore her dress and cut off her hair, crying and sobbing. She crouched beside the tipi door, almost naked, wailing and shaken with grief, gashing her body and legs with her knife until she was covered with blood. Her relatives all joined in the dismal chorus, crying and wailing, and their melancholy voices, long drawn out, rose and fell, dying away like the howling of a wolf.

This fearful sound was interrupted by the chief, who came out of the tipi, embraced his mother, and told her not to wail. "Mother," he said, "do not wail! Our boy is only sleeping!"

At that, the old woman, torn between hope and fear, followed him into the dark lodge to pass her hands over the boy that she might make sure whether he lived or died. Her eyes were in her fingers, for a film had long covered the eyes in her head.

Inside the darkened tipi, the old woman, still shaken with sobs, groped for the couch where the bundle lay, trying to find her grandson, calling to him and talking to him as only a grandmother can talk to her boy. But she could make nothing of the long bundle, though Whirlwind insisted that Little Chief lay there sleeping. Then the old woman, not knowing whether to believe her own senses or the words of her son, with her nails tore away the film from before her blind old eyes to see for herself.

But her eyes saw none the better for that agony. And when, after fumbling at the couch again, she heard the rattle of the bones within the bundle, the old woman said no more. She left the tipi and groped her way to one of the other lodges nearby. There she sat in the darkness, rocking back and forth, broken in body and spirit, sobbing with grief and pain the long night through.

The Scalp Dance still went on, and Whirlwind could hear the wild tossing of the voices on the night air, the fierce ululations, and the dull thudding of the drums above the sing-song of the musicians. The camp was quite dark, and the only fire was that about which the dancers still tirelessly circled. But when a lull in the singing came, Whirlwind stepped to the door of his tipi and shouted in the manner of a crier, naming the principal men of the camp in turn and repeating their names, inviting them to come, eat, and smoke in his tipi. He concluded his announcement by calling so that all the camp could hear, "My son invites you!"

The women, obedient to his orders, had built a fire in the kitchen and cooked a large kettle of meat for the feast. The guests were surprised and shocked by the announcement, but they dared not refuse the invitation. They came bringing their food bowls, directing their steps towards the large yellow lodge, which glowed like a great paper lantern with the light of the blazing fire within. But there was no talk among them.

When all had assembled, the women brought the kettles and passed them in. Two young men sitting near the door rose and served the food, carrying the kettles around and letting every man help himself. Not a word was spoken while the guests filled their bowls and ate the food. When all had finished, Whirlwind lighted his long-stemmed pipe. Then, taking a few puffs, he passed it to his neighbor, and all smoked together without speaking a word, passing the pipe from hand to hand.

For a time the fire blazed garishly in the center, illuminating the grave features of the naked warriors, throwing fantastic shadows on the walls behind them, and making the figure on the bed at the back of the lodge jump and struggle weirdly. But as the silent smoking went on interminably through the long night, the fire died down again, until the dark naked figures were just visible about the red pool of light in the center. The pipe bowl alternately glowed and dimmed as it was passed from hand to hand, or darkened and disappeared altogether when it was emptied and had to be refilled. Not a word was said. They could hear only the soft flapping of the tipi-covering against the poles high above their heads, the wild music of the Scalp Dance, and the broken sobbing of the old woman in the adjoining lodge.

At times the fire sank so low that it merely intensified the gloom; then someone would push a stick across the embers, and a lurid blue flame would leap up, darting its light to the very apex of the tall, conical tipi, where the poles which supported the painted covering were gathered together. It flashed its light upon the faces of the Indians, motionless as statues, upon the decorated bed and its uncanny burden, upon the weapons hung on high, and upon the bowed shoulders of the chief, who sat staring at the fire, his robe over his head. As time went on and the fire began to die indeed, Whirlwind's head sank lower and lower on his breast. The pipe ceased to circulate, for he neglected to refill it. Still his silent guests sat in the darkness without a word. The stars looked down curiously through the smoke-hole upon that silent, sombre gathering, until the darknes that precedes the dawn gave way to the first faint glimmer of the coming day.

In the gray light the watchers could see their chief, his head bowed on his breast, sitting as they had seen him last, with the stone-cold pipe in his hand. Then one of them, attracting the attention of the others, spoke to them in the silent language of signs: "My friends, let us not disturb him. Let us go away and say nothing."

So the feasters, wrapped in their white robes, left the painted tipi noiselessly, and slipped away through the gray dawn like ghosts, while a malformed moon, red and ugly, quite killed the white beauty of the morning star.

All that day Whirlwind sat in the empty lodge by the dead fire, his cold pipe in his hand, his robe over his head, without motion or stir. No one came to carry away the kettles left half-empty by his guests, for the women were afraid to go into the tipi, and the men had no desire to meddle in the affairs of their chief. Thus he sat there alone while the sun rose and passed over and set again and passed on to a new rising.

For three days and nights he sat there alone in his tipi. No one would venture in, for a man in such a mood needs slight excuse for slaughter. But Whirlwind's relatives were alarmed, because they thought he might starve to death, and they talked a great deal of going in to him. But no one went. At length, someone suggested that, if a little child were sent in to speak to him or touch him, he would respond gently and no one could be harmed. But every mother clasped her baby and said, "Not *my* child—some other!" So nothing was done.

During the fourth night, while all the camp slept, Whirlwind heard some one speak to him in the lodge. He looked up, full of anger, for he would not be disturbed in his grief. But when he saw who had spoken, his anger departed. Beside the fire sat a great bird resembling an eagle, but much larger, cloudy blue in color, with red bill and eyes, and zig-zag markings from the eyes downward over the back. Then the great bird spoke to him and said:

"My son, I am the Thunder Bird. The thunder you hear is the beating of my wings, and the lightning is the snapping of my beak and the flashing of my eyes. I am powerful. You are in trouble; your medicine is no good; your son is sleeping. But I have taken pity on you.

"My son, I am powerful. But now it is autumn. I am going away to the cave in the mountain where I have my winter lodge. You will not hear my song in the sky after today. But when you hear the first thunder in the spring, you will know that I have come back. When you hear that, take a filled pipe and go north to the Blackfeet. There is a man there in a blue tipi to whom I have given great powers. He is my servant. He will take pity on you."

Now when the great bird had finished, Whirlwind was about to thank him, for the Thunder Bird was a powerful deity. But all at once there was a great rushing of wind, and a terrible clap of thunder, so that the chief was dazed by the flash and the concussion. When he recovered, he heard the rain beating on the tipi, and far up in the sky the rolling and rumbling of the Thunder, as it winged its way westward towards the mountains where it dwelt in winter.

The rain was pouring down in torrents, but Whirlwind stepped outside his tipi and fired off his gun. Standing there, while the rain sluiced off his naked shoulders and ran down his bare legs, with

the wind whipping his sodden hair about his face, he shouted with all his might in emulation of the strom, wakening the people throughout the camp and making them listen even above the roar of the rain.

"We shall leave this place at dawn and go south of the Black Hills for the winter hunting! The Dog Soldiers will kill anyone who refuses to go when the camp is moved! Whirlwind has spoken!"

Then the people were relieved to know that their chief was himself again. But Whirlwind went back into the tipi, ate some of the stale, cold stew in the kettle, and fell into a sound sleep.

CHAPTER VIII

THE FIRST THUNDER IN THE SPRING

ACCORDING to their custom, the Cheyennes passed the winter hunting in the region south of the Black Hills. During all those dreary months of cold and darkness, Whirlwind persisted in speaking of his son as sleeping, not dead. He would not permit his relatives to mourn and in every way behaved as though Little Chief were still alive. The long bundle still reposed upon the couch in the place of honor in the painted tipi, and from time to time the chief placed a bowl of food beside it. When the camp moved, the bundle was carried on a travois drawn by the boy's pony. In time the people of the camps became accustomed to the strange behavior of their chief, and thought no more about it.

When the winter began to wane and the snow melted from the prairie, Whirlwind caused his wives to make many pairs of moccasins for him and pack them well with pemmican. It was a long march to the country of the Blackfeet—so far that the Cheyennes seldom came in contact with this people. A man would wear out many moccasins on the way, and need a plentiful supply of food. The country through which he must pass was haunted by the Sioux, the Crows, and the Snakes—all hereditary enemies of the Cheyennes. Indeed, the word "stranger" was synonymous with "enemy" anywhere on the plains. If seen, a lone man was killed without parley. He had no chance. For this reason the chief had decided to go on foot, for a mounted man could be seen at a great distance, and pony tracks were easy to find and easy to follow. It never occurred to Whirlwind to disobey his vision and remain with his own people. The Plains Indians were intensely religious.

One day the Cheyennes heard the first thunder of the spring rumbling faintly, far away towards the mountains. Then Whirlwind said, "Many Drums is calling." He took his long-stemmed pipe and filled it carefully with a mixture of tobacco and the bark of the red willow, sealing the bowl smoothly with a bit of tallow. He packed his moccasins and his meat upon the back of a strong wolf-dog, and when evening came, started north, guiding his steps by the

Star-that-never-moves. He wore only a pair of plain, brown hunting leggings, his moccasins, breech-cloth, and a buffalo robe. His quiver of panther skin hung about his shoulders, and his knife sheath was thrust into his belt behind. On his left arm he carried the pipe, and in his right hand the lance of Killer the Mandan.

He traveled by night most of the time, avoiding the trails and camps of the Indians in his path, and hiding by day in thickets, caves, or the thick timber along the streams. His route led him across many streams, large and small, all flowing east and north towards the Missouri. These he crossed, if possible, by fording, tying his belongings upon his head to keep them dry. Where the current was too swift or the water too deep for this, Whirlwind swam over, pulling his things behind him on a raft by a cord held in his teeth.

Where the indications were that no Indians were about, he traveled by day, making better time. He had been trained to observe and interpret almost automatically the calls and movements of wild animals, and knew at once when these indicated the presence of men in his neighborhood. The flight or cries of birds, the behavior of wolves and grazing herds—all these were full of meaning, and he was ever on the alert to see them. Thus, every animal he saw was a guardian and a friend. Yet he never relaxed his vigilance. He never crossed a ridge without first carefully scanning all the country as far as he could see on all sides. He never descended into a valley without a searching scrutiny for smoke or movements that might betray the presence of his enemies.

One night, after a long day's march, Whirlwind stopped beside a small stream to make camp. A storm was threatening, and he looked carefully for shelter. Just as it grew dark he found the entrance to a small cave overlooking the creek—a dry, airy, comfortable cavern, with a soft floor of loose sand. Here he spread his robe after his meal, and almost immediately fell asleep. His dog had deserted him, running off one night with the wolves. He was alone.

In the night he suddenly sat up broad awake. It was pitch dark in the cave, and there was not a sound to break the stillness. Whirlwind did not know what had wakened him at first. But soon, although his strained senses told him nothing, he *felt* that there was some one in the cave. For a long time he sat motionless, listening. The only sound was the beating of the blood in his own ears.

Finally he made out the low, regular breathing of a sleeper on his left. He carefully approached the sound, making no noise in the soft sand, until his groping fingers touched the edge of a buffalo robe, and, upon this, the warm, bare body of a man. Whirlwind passed his hands over the sleeper, feeling his belt, leggings, and body, trying to discover who was there. The sleeping man stirred and then suddenly sat up and began to feel the Cheyenne chief in the same way.

Each felt the other's hair, but that told nothing. For both wore the hair parted from forehead to nape, hanging in a long braid down either breast. On the crown of the head the slender scalp-lock was braided separately and hung down behind. Neither could tell to what tribe the other belonged, and neither was willing to betray himself by speech.

At length, Whirlwind pressed his thumb against the body of the other, and followed this gesture with the sign for a question, the two together being interpreted, "Who are you?" The other caught the idea at once, and answered by carrying the hand of the Cheyenne up to his neck and making a sweeping gesture under the chin from ear to ear—*Cutthroat!* It was the sign for Sioux!

The Sioux repeated the question, and Whirlwind, under the touch of the other's fingers, made the tribal sign for the Cheyennes, drawing his right index finger several times across his left wrist.

Then for a time the two enemies sat silent in the darkness, without moving, holding each other's hands. Neither wished to fight an unknown man in the pitchy blackness of the cave. An Indian has a strong distaste for death in the dark. They agreed to lie down there in the cave and wait for morning before taking any action. All this they arranged in the sign talk, feeling one another's fingers, as some old man, blind and deaf, talks with his relatives in the camps. Then they lay down there side by side in the darkness of the little cave and waited for the dawn.

At daybreak, the two men got up and looked at each other. Whirlwind was surprised to find that his bedfellow was little more than a boy. He had seemed much larger in the dark. Now the chief saw that he was hardly bigger than Little Chief. They ate their food and then talked together in the sign language. It was agreed that they would not fight, but would wager their scalps upon a contest in shooting. Each was to shoot four arrows at a mark, and the winner was to have the other's scalp.

Whirlwind took his bow from the quiver of panther skin and strung it, testing the twisted sinew string with his finger. It was a beautiful weapon, made of the dark, polished wood of the Osage orange, strong enough to send an arrow through a buffalo cow so that the head projected a hand's breadth on the other side. He tested the spring of his bow once or twice, and then, putting an arrow on the string, loosed it high in the air so that, when it fell, it stood upright in a level patch of buffalo grass beyond the creek. This was the mark. Each one shot four arows at it in turn. Then they crossed the creek together to see the result of their shooting.

Before they reached the spot, the young Sioux saw that he had lost. His arrows were well bunched about the mark, but he could not compete with a veteran warrior and hunter like the Cheyenne chief. Whirlwind's arrows had fallen so close that two of his shafts actually touched the mark. The boy had lost the wager.

The young Sioux threw down his quiver and his

knife. He was trembling, but controlled himself. He knelt down on the grass, facing the Cheyenne, and bowed his head for the ordeal. Whirlwind looked at the boy, waiting there, ready for the knife. A brave boy, he thought. Little Chief would have done the same. It was a pity, but the boy was a Sioux, and a scalp is a scalp. The Cheyenne drew his long keen blade from its sheath, and stepped towards the Sioux. He took the slender braid of the scalp-lock in his hand.

Scalping was not necessarily fatal. Many men have lived a lifetime after such an ordeal. But when the young man felt the sharp steel touch his flesh, his control gave way. He jumped suddenly to his feet, and his short, oiled braid slipped through the clumsy fingers of the Cheyenne chief, scarred and stiffened since the fight with Ironshirt. The boy jumped back and faced the chief, raising one hand.

"Wait," he said. "I am a Sioux. You have won. But I want to live. I give you my body and my weapons. I give you the right to count the coup. Let me go! All my family have been killed by the Cheyennes. I am the only man left!"

Whirlwind placed one foot on the boy's quiver, where it lay on the grass, and picked up his own bow. The boy could not escape him. But he was curious to know his story, and to learn what the Sioux had to say of his own prowess as a fighter. Using the Sioux tongue, he said, "Tell me about it."

This was the boy's story: "My father was called Ironshirt. He was chief. He went to the Cheyenne camp carrying the pipes of peace, but the Cheyennes broke his medicine in the camp, and then killed him. I was not there. I was sick. But all my brothers were killed in the same fight. There were only my grandfather, One Horn, and I.

"When my grandfather came back, we all mourned for my father and my brothers. We gave away all that we had and cut our hair. My grandfather sat all day in the lodge, grieving for his son. He was no good. He became a feeble old man. We were poor. No one cared what became of us.

"One day in the fall of the year, my grandfather met Two Crows coming from a council of the chiefs. My grandfather stopped Two Crows and said, 'Where are you going to hunt this winter?' For Two Crows became head chief after my father was killed. The chief Two Crows hated the sight of the old man, because he had caused the death of his brother-friend. So he answered, 'What is that to you? You are too old and worn out to go along. You cannot travel. We shall leave you on the prairie for the wolves to eat.'

"My grandfather laughed and answered, 'I am a medicine man and a chief. You cannot get along without me.' The old man thought Two Crows was joking.

"But Two Crows said, 'I do not want to see you around any more. You threw an iron spoon into the stew that Ironshirt ate in the Cheyenne camp. That broke his medicine. I told him to keep out of the fight because his medicine was no good. But you sent him to his death. Who wants an old man around who has killed his only son?'

"When my grandfather heard that, he said no more. Before Two Crows spoke, the old man had not known that he had caused my father's death. He sat in his tipi, wrapped in his robe, saying nothing, eating his heart. All that day and the following night he sat there. No one dared speak to him. But in the morning the old man came out of his tipi, mounted his horse, and rode out through the camp, shouting that he would kill the first living thing that crossed his path. No one dared to stand in his way, for he had his weapons. We knew he was frantic with grief.

"He rode off across the prairie, and after a while I followed him and looked over the ridge he had crossed. When I got there, the old man was riding around an old buffalo bull, shooting arrows into it. It was the time when the bulls are fiercest, running alone and fighting fiercely among themselves, stopping for nothing. When this bull felt the arrows in its side, it charged my grandfather time after time, but always the pony managed to get out of the way. When the old man saw that he could not make the horse face the infuriated bull, he jumped off the pony and drove it away, shooting arrows into its flanks. The horse ran back to the camp with the arrows sticking in its hide, and the men there began to catch their ponies and come out to see what the matter was.

"My grandfather was an old man, armed only

The Fight Between One Horn and the Buffalo Bull

with his knife, but when the bull charged him, he managed to keep clear of its sharp horns, and stabbed it as it passed. The more they fought, the fiercer the bull became. It charged and charged, turning and swinging its great head quick as a flash. The bull was very quick on its feet. It did not shut its eyes to charge, but followed every turn of its enemy. But the old man was full of insane strength and cunning, and managed for a long time to keep away from his huge antagonist. But at last the bull caught my grandfather and tossed him high in the air, goring and trampling him when he fell until the old man had no life in him.

"When the men saw the bull toss my grandfather, they charged down at it and tried to drive it away, shooting arrows into it. But the bull would not leave the body, and stood over it, bleeding and bellowing, swinging its head from side to side and jumping about, until it too fell dead from the wounds of my grandfather's knife.

"That was the death of my grandfather! My father is dead! My brothers are dead! Let me go!"

Whirlwind stood watching the Sioux boy, his foot on the boy's quiver, his knife in hand. Surely enough men had died on account of the Mandan, save *one*. This boy was brave, a fine boy—like Little Chief, he thought with a pang. The story of One Horn's grief touched him. Moreover, the bravest deed of all was held to be the release of an enemy, when absolutely at the mercy of his captor. Men had been made chiefs for such deeds. Whirlwind stooped to pick up the boy's knife. He would keep this as evidence of his exploit. Then he sheathed his own.

"Young man," he said, "the Mandans have caused all this trouble, not the Cheyennes. I want you to offer four Mandan scalps to the Sun. If you will do this, I will let you go."

Then the boy said, "*Ho!* I will do it," and stroked the arms of Whirlwind, thanking and blessing him for sparing his life. They gathered up their arrows and walked away, the boy eastward towards his people's country, the Cheyenne to the northwest towards the country of the Blackfeet. When they reached the tops of the hills on either side of the creek, they stopped and raised their hands to each other, as they had agreed. Henceforth, their truce was at an end.

Whirlwind went on and on, day after day, without meeting any Indians. However, he was not lonely. Almost always he was within sight of wild animals—elk moving along, waving their leaflike ears and grazing through the bottoms in large groups; bears grubbing in the underbrush; antelopes in long lines turning and facing like troops at drill in imitation of every movement of the leading buck, or fading wraithlike over the plains at the first breath of alarm; wolves by ones and twos, leading him to game, or following patiently behind in hopes of a share in the next kill; deer feeding along the streams, and fleeing with upraised, flashing tails as he approached; coyotes trotting along the ridges; eagles among the treetops and about the lofty buttes; and all the myriad smaller creatures that burrowed, dived, or flew in the free earth, water, and air of the bountiful plains. All these animals were the man's friends, providing him warning, food, and—in his dreams—advice.

For days he passed over great plains where enormous herds of buffalo—each one made up of many smaller herd—moved slowly across his path. Their quiet gait and calm demeanor assured him that no Indians had recently disturbed them. They surrounded him on all sides as far as he could see, covering the plain as it were with one great buffalo robe. The prairies were black with them, and the sound of their lowing and bellowing was ever in his ears. All the streams were so fouled by their passage that a man could not swallow the water. Day and night they moved past, and Whirlwind was compelled to make his bed under fallen logs in the timber to save himself from their trampling hoofs. All night long he could hear that vast sea of huge animals moving by, crashing through the underbrush about him and pushing their great, shaggy sides against the logs under which he had taken refuge until the trunks and branches above his head were brown with their shed wool. He was glad to pass through the herds, for he knew that their hoofs would soon obliterate his own trail and prevent anyone from following him.

For many days Whirlwind moved steadliy northwest, crossing stream after stream, keeping the mountains always on his left. He crossed the Dry

Fork of the Cheyenne River, followed up Black Thunder Creek, crossed the Belle Fourche, Powder River, and Tongue River—where the Big Horn Mountains loomed on the near horizon. He crossed the Little Big Horn, the Big Horn, and the Yellowstone. He swam the Musselshell and waded the headwaters of the many small streams that drain towards the Missouri north of it. At last he saw the dark massed timber and shining levels of the Missouri itself, and crossed it too, not without difficulty, within sound of the great falls. Beyond this he knew nothing of the country, and advanced with the utmost caution.

As he went on he found the country an ideal range for buffalo and Indians—a noble, boundless, gently rolling plain, punctuated at long intervals by isolated buttes or groups of hills, well watered by many streams, and dominated on the west by the towering snow-capped summits of the Rockies. Beaver swarmed along the streams, choking them with their dams and lodges. Buffalo were plenty. Game of all kinds was abundant, and Whirlwind threw away the remnant of dried meat which he had saved during the earlier stages of his journey. With such a range as this, it was not surprising that the Blackfeet had so increased in numbers and power as to be the terror of the northern plains. Whirlwind went on cautiously, living on the fat of the land.

One night, as he was walking over the rolling, starlit prairie, his nostrils caught the faint, acrid odor of burning buffalo chips. Following up-wind, he found the scent growing stronger and stronger until he crossed a ridge and saw in the little valley before him the thick, dark foliage which marked the bed of a creek. He advanced noiselessly and crossed the dry, caked bed of the little stream. Beyond it the ground was studded with small clumps of low bushes, torn by washouts, and deeply scarred by old buffalo trails. Whirlwind had no difficulty in creeping out of the stream-bed under cover. Some little distance from the stream, beneath a group of old trees, he saw a fire vaguely smoking into the night air and faintly illuminating the dark trunks and pale green foliage of the cottonwoods. Around the fire he counted eleven figures wrapped in buffalo robes, all apparently sound asleep. This was evidently a war party, worn out by a long ride and camping, as usual when no danger was anticipated, without a guard. In the prairie beyond the fire, Whirlwind could make out a herd of grazing ponies. Were the men Blackfeet? Or Crows? Who were they? Friends or enemies? For a long time the Cheyenne lay watching.

Suddenly one of the sleepers stirred and got up, and Whirlwind saw the peculiar, high pompadour, stiffened with grease and red clay, which was the distinguishing mark of his enemies the Crows. He lay quiet in his concealment until the man had returned to his bed and was apparently asleep. Then he silently withdrew, made a circuit, and came out on the prairie among the ponies. He quietly loosed those which were picketed, mounted one of them, and gradually urged the herd away from the camp. He lay flat on his pony's back, so that, if one of the sleepers should awake, his own figure would not be seen. When he had eased the herd over the hill, out of sight of the camp, he rounded them up and urged them into a trot and then into a run. The animals seemed used to running together, and made him little trouble. He was thoroughly tired of walking, and his moccasins were nearly gone. It was good to feel a horse beneath him again.

All night he rode hard, driving the herd before him. When morning came he found he had more than fifty head, many of them fine animals with eagle feathers in their tails. Soon after, he crossed a stream and found the site of a recently deserted camp of twenty lodges. The ashes of some of the lodge-fires still contained warm embers, and the sign left behind told his trained eye that the camp had not been moved more than three days. He found a discarded moccasin and its cut and the shape of its sole told him that the camp had been Blackfoot.

There was no good grass near the campsite, for the Blackfoot ponies had grazed it down. Whirlwind drove his ponies along the broad trail of the moving camp to the next valley, where he allowed his horses to graze while he slept in a nearby thicket. That afternoon he went on, following the trail of the Blackfoot camp until it became too dark to do so. It was a plain trail, for the tall grass had been beaten down by the feet of the horses when the soil was soft with rain. Here and there one of the great bare ant hills betrayed the direction of the march where a travois or a bunch of tipi poles had been dragged across it yielding surface. It was easy to follow. Early next morning he went on, and at noon that day found the trail he was following merge with that of a much larger camp, which swung to the left and passed over a ridge ahead.

Whirlwind drove his herd into the timber in the valley where he was and reconnoitered. Riding up almost to the top of the ridge, he dismounted and crept to the top to look over. Before him was spread a wide valley through which ran a river, marked by shining stretches of water and broad masses of dark green foliage. Beyond the river the bluffs rose steeply, studded with rocks. Far beyond them towered the majesic snow-clad barriers of the Great Shining Mountains, the Rockies. On this side of the river, in a level, grassy plain covered with innumerable horses, stood a great double camp circle of smoking tipis. The Blackfeet had assembled for their summer festival.

The Cheyenne chief crept back to his horse and rode down to the timber where he had left the herd of ponies. There he dismounted, stripped, and washed himself in the creek. He opened a paint pouch and covered his entire body with white earth paint, such as was worn by a mourner. Under each eye he painted a tiny crooked black mark to represent a tear. He loosened his long hair about his

shoulders, and put on his breechcloth. All his other clothing and belongings he hid in the underbrush. Thus arrayed as a suppliant, he took the long-stemmed pipe, mounted a horse, and rode towards the Blackfoot camp, driving the herd before him.

The Blackfoot camp was very large. It contained more than five hundred tipis, and measured more than a mile across the circle. Within the large outer circle was a much smaller one made up of the tipis of the chiefs of the warrior orders. These tipis were the headquarters of the organizations which controlled the camp.

As Whirlwind rode into the camp, he began to wail and cry with a loud voice, moving slowly around the circle, driving the ponies before him, and looking for the blue tipi of which the Thunder Bird had spoken. As he passed, the people came running out of their lodges to see him. Painted as he was with white clay, almost naked, his loose hair hanging about his shoulders, without a weapon or a distinguishing mark of any kind, they could not tell who he was or to what tribe he belonged. They stood watching him, hand over mouth in token of surprise. He paid no attention to the people, but rode on, wailing and crying and carefully inspecting every painted tipi in the hope of finding the man he had come so many weary miles to see.

There were many tipis in the camp painted with ancient protective designs to insure good fortune to their occupants. The designs were quite different from those of other tribes, some of them very striking. No two were alike. Most were painted at the top with crosses and disks representing stars on a dark ground. At the bottom of the tent a dark band represented the earth, and between top and bottom the space was usually of a lighter color, and bore representations of animals, rainbows, rocks, and other natural phenomena. Of these, the figures of the buffalo and otter were most frequently seen. As Whirlwind passed round the circle, he scanned each tipi carefully, but always he was disappointed. None of these tipis was blue. None carried the picture of the Thunder Bird.

He had almost completed the circuit of the camp, when he saw, a short distance ahead, a large, handsome tipi—the Thunder Tipi. Above, it was blue—dark as a thunder cloud and without stars. Next to the ground the tipi was painted with a wide red band topped with a sawtooth edge representing mountains, the home of the Thunder. The space between top and bottom was a peculiar light blue, marked off from the deeper color above by a red zigzag line encircling the tent and representing the lightning trail of the Thunder. At the back of the lodge near the bottom, was a yellow disk some two feet in diameter, and on this was painted the Thunder Bird in blue, with wings outspread and red lightning flashing from its head. Behind the tipi, on a tripod, hung the drum and medicine bundle which belonged to it. Nearby, under a shelter, three or four Indians sat in the shade.

Whirlwind got off his horse and began to wail louder than ever when he saw this tipi, holding the stem of his pipe towards the painted Thunder Bird. There he remained, crying and wailing, while the Blackfeet watched him curiously from their lodge doors. After a while a man came from the shelter and, emphasizing his meaning with a gesture, said, "Come."

Whirlwind followed the man to the shelter and took his seat in the shade. On a buffalo robe, propped up on pillows of whitened deerskin, lay an old, old man. He wore only a breechcloth, and his daughter, herself an old woman, sat there keeping the flies off his shriveled body with a brush made from the tail of a buffalo. Whirlwind thought he had never before seen a man so old. The flesh had shrunk away from his gaunt frame, leaving the joints standing out like wrinkled knobs on the gnarled limbs. His hands were like talons. The skin of his face, withered and furrowed, sagged about his sunken eyes and toothless mouth. His sparse hair, coarse and short, hung over his stooping shoulders, white as snow. But the eyes burned in their deep sockets with a strong and eager flame.

For some time the old man stared searchingly at his visitor. Then, slowly and with precision, he asked in the sign language why he came wailing to the Thunder Tipi. Then Whirlwind told why he had come, and what the Thunder Bird had promised. The Blackfeet covered their mouths with astonishment when they learned that their visitor was a Cheyenne who had come on foot a march of thirty "sleeps" to find their tipi. But the old man gave no sign, though his fiery eyes burned more fiercely as the chief told of the vision and how the Thunder Bird had sent him to its servant. When Whirlwind had finished his story, he added, earnestly, "Grandfather, I give you all these ponies. Take pity on me!"

The old man shifted himself a little on his cushions, and after a time began to speak in the language of signs, slowly indeed, but without fumbling or uncertainty.

"My son, I have been expecting you. Sixty-four winters ago, a wonderful thing happened to me. I was a grown man then, with a son who had gone on the warpath. We were camped on Two Medicine Lake in the mountains. There were four tipis. It was early summer. But one day a great snowstorm swept down from the peaks. The young people thought it was great fun, and played in the snow, throwing it at one another and wrestling naked in the drifts. I had come out of the lodge, for it was strange to see the snow falling in summer.

"While I stood there, watching the children play-ing in the snow, suddenly a large bird came flutter-ing down out of the storm and fell to the ground near my tipi, crying and beating the snow with its wings. It was a big bird—with green talons and feathers all the colors of the rainbow. Its eyes and bill were red. The young people began to pelt it with snow, chasing it around among the lodges. When I saw that I tried to stop them. I said, 'My friends, there is something mysterious about that bird. It is not like other birds. You had better not annoy it.' When I said this, they became frightened and left the bird alone. But one boy said, 'I am not afraid.' He ran after the bird, throwing snow at it and shouting as it flopped along the ground ahead of him.

"Just outside the camp was the framework of a sweat-lodge where I had been taking a sweat-bath to purify myself. The bird ran out to this lodge with the boy after it. Four times it ran around the sweat-lodge and then fell down at the entrance, crying and beating its wings. Then I knew that the bird was mysterious, and I drove the boy away. I took my robe, and asking the bird to take pity on me, threw the robe over it and caught it. When I took it up in my arms it did not cry any longer, but lay quiet, closing its eyes. It was a large bird, larger than any eagle, and had red zigzag markings from its eyes down the back. When I saw that, I was afraid. I knew then that it was the Thunder Bird.

"I called to my relatives and told them to heat

stones and bring a covering for the sweat-lodge. When everything was ready, I went into the lodge with the bird and took a sweat-bath. When I sprinkled the water on the hot stones, the bird got up an ran around the lodge four times, and then lay still on the ground. I stayed in the lodge a long time in the hot steam, praying and asking the bird to have pity on me, and singing songs of the Thunder.

"Then the bird spoke: 'My son, you protected me. I am the Thunder Bird. I am powerful, but the snow-storms overcome me. My son, I have taken pity on you. You will live long and be a great medicine man, as you desire. Warriors will come from afar to get the shields that you shall make. You shall make one shield every four years in the way which I will show you. Sixteen shields you shall make, and then you will die. Now the storm is over. Open the lodge.'

"When I raised the covering of the sweat-lodge, the storm was over and the snow was melting fast in the bright sunshine. I carried the bird out of the camp and left it in the meadow by the lake. I never saw it again. All the children who chased the bird that day died the same summer—before the next Sun Dance. But I have lived sixty-four winters since that day. I have made fifteen shields as the Thunder taught me. Cree, Sarsi, Sioux, Blackfoot, and Blood —they all came to me for their shields, and I gave them powerful protection. They could not be killed in battle. And now you have come, and it is time to make the sixteenth shield. When I have done that, I shall die."

The old man paused, tapping the ground with the long carved pipe-tamper he held in his hand. Then he went on:

"My son, I am an old man. I cannot be buried on the prairie. My dreams are of the mountains. My people are about to make the Sun Dance. I do not wish to die before I see this dance. When it is over, I will make your shield."

Then Thunder Maker took the long-stemmed pipe which Whirlwind had brought, and smoked it, thus pledging himself before the Sun to do as he had said. Whirlwind thanked the old man, stroking his arms and face, blessing him because he was ready to do this thing.

The Cheyenne chief was made welcome in the Blackfoot camp, for most of the horses he had brought into camp belonged there, having been stolen by the Crows but a few days before. Thunder Maker at once restored these animals to their owners. Whirlwind was feasted in many tipis.

Ten days later, when the Sun Dance was over, the camp broke up and every band went away to its favorite camping ground. At dawn the great circle of tipis stood intact, every tent trim and taunt on its staunch poles. Soon after, the coverings flapped in the wind as the tents were struck, and at sunrise the campsite was deserted except for the hungry dogs which nosed about among the smoking lodge-fires.

Thunder Maker and his immediate family—four tipis—moved northwards towards the mountains. The old man, though eager and alert in spirit, was much too feeble to ride a horse. He was carried in a travois made comfortable with many buffalo robes and soft cushions, with a canopy over his head to keep off the sun. They traveled by easy stages north and west along the edge of those sheer mountains which rise so abruptly from the plains. Day after day they rode leisurely on, crossing the clear, swift streams and rolling prairies, until at last they turned in towards the mountains around the head of a lake[1] which pushed out towards the plains.

Following its northwest shore, they passed into a wonderland of tumbled mountains masses, lakes and forests, cirques and glaciers, barren snowfields and meadows gorgeous with massed wild flowers. Whirlwind had never been among the mountains before, and looked with wonder at the strangely colored rocks—red, and yellow, and blue-gray, fading far ahead into the deep blues and purples of the distant divide. There for the first time he saw the mountain goat scrambling among the crags, and heard the marmot whistle from the rocks.

For miles the trail led through green, inviting forests, from which they caught glimpses of great peaks ahead, and below the rocky slopes on their left had vistas of the fairest of mountain lakes shin-

[1] The lake now know as St. Mary's Lake, in Glacier National Park.

ing in the sun. Then all at once they left the fragrant pines and came out upon a little plateau perched on a steep promontory thrust out into the lake, fully one hundred feet above the water.[2] Here they halted.

The view was sublime. Down the lake, past the narrows, the forest-clad hills slipped away towards the plains, hemming in the stately crescent of the lake with sloping, rocky shores. To the west, the deep, green water was framed by five stupendous peaks rising from its shores almost a mile in air. The lower slopes wore all the lovely greens of grass and pines, while far above, the bare rocky summits, flecked and patched with snow, showed wonderful shades of red and purplish gray.

Thunder Maker was in his glory. He loved the

[2] Now the site of Going-to-the-Sun Chalets, in Glacier National Park.

mountains, for they were the home of his bene-
factor, who had given him long life and many
honors. Most of the Plains Indians shunned the
mountains. Many were their tales of hunters lost
there and of the marvels they had seen. But the old
man was not afraid. He rejoiced to be beside the
lake again and to feel the cool breezes from the
snowfields and glaciers play upon his brow. While
the tipis were being pitched, he sat on a pile of
buffalo robes, looking up at the great red and gray
mass of the magnificent peak which towered above
the camp, and singing sonorous songs in honor of
the mountains and of the Thunder which made
them its home. Many winters of reverent contem-
plation of the wonders of Nature had given the old
man something of the dignity and grandeur of the
everlasting hills, and his spirited songs, full of deep
religious feeling and intoned with all the force of
his enthusiasm, seemed a fitting expression of the
solemnity of that noble scene.

When he had finished singing, he beckoned to
Whirlwind, and said, in the language of signs, "My
son, do you see that mountain so high above us? It
is mysterious, sacred. There the Thunder Bird has
his nest. Long ago the Sun sent one called Na'pi to
help the Blackfeet. In those days we were just like
animals. We knew nothing. Na'pi taught my people
to make tipis, to tan hides and make weapons to
defend themselves with. All that the Blackfeet
know, Na'pi taught them. For many winters he
lived among us—long, long ago. Then from this

mountain he went back to the Sun who had sent him. But his face was placed on the mountain forever, so that the Blackfeet might remember his teachings. Do you see that great snow face with the warbonnet, high up on the side of the mountain?

"That is the face of Na'pi. He placed it there when he was going to the Sun."

The old man's eyes were fixedly staring up at the snow face on that majestic peak, placed there forever beyond the reach of death and change, high up among the clouds. At last he sighed and turned to his guest. "My son, I shall soon go also. Tomorrow I make your shield."

After the evening meal the old man sat in silence for a long time watching the shadows deepen in the valley and creep up the sides of the ruddy peaks, while the wind soughed in the pine-tops and ruffled the quiet surface of the water below him. One by one the others dropped off to sleep around the fire, but all night long Thunder Maker sat facing the dark bulk of the mountain, outlined against the stars, where Na'pi had left his everlasting face. He was alone with the Mysterious Powers, hearing only the lap-lapping of the water against the rocks and the soft whispers of the wind among the pines.

Next morning the mists lay low about the green bases of the mountains, and one might have supposed that the lake rested among the rich green hills of another region. Then the wind sprang up, the mists lifted, and through the rifts could be seen

the glowing splendors of that superb peak, shining
in the morning sun. When the mists had gone,
clouds passed over in great, fleecy masses, throwing their deep shadows upon the glorious summits,
the changing verdure of the lower slopes, and the
chill green of the water, working magic transforma-
tions in their gorgeous coloring. Light blue became
deep purple, glowing red paled to faint rose with
the shifting light, which seemed to render the spectacular outlines of the distant peaks more fantastic
than before.

That morning, the blue Thunder Tipi was set up
with appropriate ceremonies in order that there
might be fair weather during the making of the
shield. The design of this tipi had been given to the
old man in a vision, and when it was pitched with
due ceremony, fine weather always resulted. So the
women pitched it now as he directed.

That done, Thunder Maker had his buffalo robe
spread beside the tipi, and brought out his medicine
bundle and drum. He took a large disk of tough bull
hide, hardened in the fire, and covered this with a
somewhat larger disk of soft white buckskin, drawing it tight by means of a throng passed through
slits all round the edge. The entire surface of the
shield he painted a bright yellow, indicating a clear
sky, and upon this background the Thunder Bird
in blue with wings displayed and red lightning
flashing from its head. He attached eagle feathers
to the shield, for the eagle lives in the mountains
and is familiar with the Thunder. Over all this he

placed a neat cover of plain white buckskin to keep the sacred designs from profane view. All this took several hours, and was attended with much ceremony. The old man gave the shield to Whirlwind, and instructed him, telling him how he must care for the shield, and teaching him the four songs that belonged to it. He also gave him certain paints and the dried skin of a swallow.

"My son," he said, "tie this swallow in your hair when you go into a fight. This is the swallow which flies about just before a thunderstorm. He is closely related to the Thunder Bird. He is agile. You must paint your horse with red lightning along the legs, and he will be as agile as the swallow. Now I have given you all my medicine. You will be a great warrior. The Mandans will not be able to stand before you. But one thing more is necessary. We must take a sweat together. The sweat-bath makes men brave."

They went into the close, hot sweat-lodge and took the steam bath together, singing songs of the Thunder and fulfilling all the rites of the final ceremony of purification. When the coverings of the sweat-lodge were taken off the framework, the old man said, "Now we shall go down to the lake and take a plunge."

Then his relatives tried to dissuade him, saying that he was too old to go into the chill waters of the lake, all dripping with perspiration as he was. But Thunder Maker was firm. "For sixty-four winters," he said, "I have followed the instructions of the

Thunder, and I have never been sick! I will not disregard his words now!"

The old man was so indignant that he would not allow them to help him down the steep, rocky path that led to the lake. He crept down himself, past ledges thick with tufted fern and saxifrage, and jumped off into the ice-green waters. Whirlwind himself was chilled through by the plunge, and the shock was too great for the old man. He succumbed at once, and would have drowned before their eyes if the Cheyenne chief had not carried him ashore. They hastily wrapped him in a buffalo robe and carried him, half-conscious, to the fire. It was some time before the warmth revived him.

When it did, he asked to be propped up a little. He told them all that his time had come, as it had been foretold, and gave instructions for his burial. The others took his best clothing from the bags and dressed him in it with loving care. They anointed his face with the blue thunder paint, and brought his pipe and medicine bundle to lay beside him. When all had been done to his satisfaction, the old man beat with trembling hand upon the drum, and looking out of the tipi towards the lofty peak which he venerated, sang in a clear, thin voice his death-song—a plaintive melody with many vocables and these few words:

"Only the mountains endure!"

At evening they carried him out and laid him, wrapped in the blue cover of the Thunder Tipi, upon a high point of rock on the little promontory, where the view of the mountain was most sublime. Over the grave they raised a cairn of stones, and around this at each of the four cardinal points a buffalo skull was placed.

While they were still at work the Thunder began to growl in the mountains, and as they hurried away to their camping place, the lightning flashed above their heads, lighting up the great snow face and playing about the peak. The rain began to fall, slowly at first, and then in torrents, darkening the green surface of the lake, while the wind struck the tall pines with a force that made them bend and

groan. The Indians did not wait for the storm to stop, but broke camp and hurried away to the plains, fleeing from that solemn sepulchre, where the cold face of Na'pi watched from his sublime crag, and the rolling drums of the Thunder sounded the requiem of his priest.

CHAPTER IX

THE MANDAN VILLAGE

WHEN Whirlwind left the Blackfeet, he went down
the stream on which they were camped until he
came to the Missouri. Crossing the river, he followed its course eastward, traveling by night
through the country of the Assiniboines and Gros
Ventres. These tribes were deadly enemies of the
Cheyennes. But Whirlwind never relaxed his
watchfulness, and came at last to Knife River and
the country of the Mandans. It was nearly morning
when he crossed this stream. He made camp on
the south bank and slept through the day. The
Blackfeet had told him that the Mandan village
was only a few miles below.

When night came again, Whirlwind ate his evening meal in the shadows of the timber, watching the great red moon rise behind the bluffs and throw a copper chain across the shimmering waters of the Missouri. When he had finished, he took a glowing coal from his tiny fire, and placing it before him on the cleared ground, laid upon it a short braid of dried sweetgrass. As the fragrant white smoke rose through the quiet air, he stood over it with his robe held loosely about him, so that the incense passed over the whole surface of his body. Thus purified, he anointed his face with the blue paint given him by Thunder Maker, removed the white cover from the shield the old man had made, and tied the swallow skin in his hair. Then he sang the four prescribed Songs of the Thunder. Thus Whirlwind prayed for success in revenging the death of his son.

The ritual over, he covered the shield, took his weapons, and walked downstream. He avoided the timber and set out over the open prairie, wearing his whitened buffalo robe tied about his waist and shrouding his head as well. In the timber he might blunder upon some Indians in the darkness. In the open he felt secure in his white robe. The moon was so bright on the prairie that a white object simply disappeared at a distance and was blurred to indistinctness even close by. If seen at all, he would be taken for a wolf scampering on the plains. Many a time on the warpath he had scouted thus on the moonlit prairies.

For several hours he walked slowly over the

gentle, grassy swells within easy distance of the stream, looking for the home of his enemy. Towards morning he saw, perched high upon a bluff overhanging the river, the dark, confused blur of the Mandan village. Whirlwind turned towards the river. It was useless to prowl through the sleeping town in the hope of finding his victim. People would soon be up and about, and in daylight a stranger was sure to be detected. The prairie offered no cover. His plan was to find some hiding place nearby where he could watch the village and the trails leading from it, and perhaps waylay Killer outside the palisade.

Less than half a mile above the village he found the level prairie dropping steeply away some twenty feet, the bank thus formed enclosing a wide amphitheatre almost level with the water of the river flowing past. This space was overgrown with tall, lush grass and growths of willow, with here and there a little patch of Indian corn cultivated by the Mandans. A well-beaten trail crossed it, coming from the river and climbing the hill towards the village. The Cheyenne slipped down this bank, and walked out upon the level. He found a thick clump of willows near the trail, and near enough to the river to give him a good view of the village on the bluff downstream. There he made himself comfortable and slept until sunrise.

He was awakened by the patter of feet on the trail, and looking out, saw crowds of women coming down to the river with their water-jars, laughing and chattering. As they approached the river, they put down their jars, and throwing off their clothing, walked to the brink and plunged in, splashing and shouting and shrieking with laughter. They swam well and fearlessly and played all manner of tricks, thoroughly enjoying their frolic. This was their daily custom, and soon almost the whole feminine population of the village was on the beach or in the water. Well back from the river on the upper terrace Whirlwind could see a number of warriors mounted and fully armed, keeping guard over the bathing place.

Suddenly the women began to scream and shout louder than ever. An old woman had launched one of the clumsy, tublike bull-boats or coracles that lay along the shore, and was laboriously paddling across the stream on some errand to the other bank. She sat in the middle, thrusting the paddle down into the water in the direction in which she wished to go, and pulling it towards her with short, quick strokes, making the unwieldy little craft move slowly over the surface. Her boat was hemispherical in shape, made of a raw hide stretched over a framework of willow sticks.

Some of the swimmers, seeing what she was about, had gathered around her and taken hold of the little craft. In spite of the pleas and threats of the old woman, they began spinning it round and round as on a pivot, to the intense amusement of all who saw it. The helpless old woman, precariously perched upon her baggage in the bottom of the tub, screamed and scolded at the top of her voice, striking at the knuckles of her tormentors with the paddle. But where one hand was forced to release the boat, a dozen others seized it. The blows fell harmlessly upon the gunwale, and all her outcry was in vain. They spun her round and round, faster and faster, until the dizzy old creature gave up all effort to prevent their antics, and allowed her helpless craft to drift with the swift current. When at last they left her, she resumed her paddling and landed in time on the other shore, far below her objective. In such manner the women, according to their daily custom, amused themselves during the bathing hour.

After a time they began to fill their water-jars and come out of the stream to dress. Singly and in small groups they passed up the trail to the village, carrying their jars, chattering and laughing like children. Whirlwind might easily have killed numbers of them. This would have been considered a brave deed under the circumstances, for it would have called down the immediate attack of all the men in the village. But Whirlwind was on another errand, and let them pass within the length of his lance, unharmed.

When most of the women had left the river, suddenly the Cheyenne saw a young man, very carefully and handsomely dressed coming down the path from the village. He strutted deliberately along, carefully keeping his finery from the touch of the dewy grass and willows along the trail, the

embroidered flaps of his fancy moccasins trailing a
yard behind his ankles. He had left his spotted pony
on the terrace above, but from his wrist dangled his
carved quirt of elkhorn with its lash of knotted
bull's hide, his buffalo tail fly-brush, his mirror in
its decorated wooden frame. His hair was elaborately dressed and anointed, with long pendants of
beads and twisted wire hanging from either temple
to his waist, and a crest of swansdown and irides-
cent duck feathers above. His face, screened by the
fan of turkey feathers which he held in his right
hand, was elaborately painted with vermilion and
yellow. Large metal bangles hung from the lobes

and cartilage of his ears, and a necklace encircled
his throat. Under one arm he carried a thick bundle
of sticks, painted red, the tally of his conquests
among the Mandan women. A lover's flute pro-
truded from the hand which grasped his robe.
Whirlwind recognized the type at once. Indian
dandies were not unknown even among the warlike, nomadic Cheyennes, but the Mandans' sedentary, village life produced them in numbers and to
perfection. Whirlwind looked at the fellow with
all the contempt which a true warrior felt for a fop
whose hands had never gripped the scalping knife
and whose head had never been decorated with the
hard-won quills of the war eagle. Here was a pro-
fessional lover going to meet some woman as she
came from the river.

The young man halted near Whirlwind's hiding
place, standing aside from the path to let the
woman pass, and blocking the chief's view of the
path towards the river. Presently a woman came
along, and the young man stepped into the path
before her. She set down her water-jar and waited.
The dandy advanced, and with a sweeping gesture
of his arm threw his robe around her, covering her
head. They stepped back into the thicket where
Whirlwind lay, and almost trod upon him. He
remained motionless, scarcely breathing, watching
the lovers fondle one another, his knife ready in his
hand. How easily he could have killed them both!

Often and often he had lain thus all day on the
top of some tall butte in a pit covered with green

boughs, waiting for the eagles whose feathers he coveted, his bait the stuffed hide of a coyote lined with rich red meat. Droll strutting magpies and greedy crows might come to his hiding place to peck and hop about the trap, but he would have nothing to do with them. Let them go. He waited for the eagle which he could see circling far above in the sky, scanning the bait for trickery, circling nearer and nearer, until the great bird alighted upon the hilltop and approached the bait, walking out upon the boughs which masked the pit. Then he had reached through the boughs and quickly grasped the scaly talons, drawing the bird down into the pit and breaking its neck for its feathers. In like manner he waited now, indifferent to fops and women, for the murderer of his son.

The lovers stood in the thicket, caressing one another, and talking in a language which Whirlwind could not understand. So near they stood that he gently touched them both, and the heavy perfume of the dandy nearly choked him. The long, elaborately decorated flap of the man's moccasin lay near his hand, and Whirlwind cut it off noiselessly with his knife, to keep as evidence of the coup. How easily he might have killed them! But he was out for bigger game.

At length they heard the sound of the watchers on the terrace shouting to the last of the women to hurry. Then the lovers stepped back into the path, and the young dandy walked slowly away like a strutting turkey cock, nimbly fanning himself and paying no further attention to the woman. She stooped to take up her water-jar. The robe slipped from her head. Whirlwind almost forgot his caution; he half rose from the thicket, and his knuckles stood out bleakly round the knife haft. It was A-nu'tah!

All day long Whirlwind crouched in his hiding place waiting for the enemy that never came. The covert he had chosen was in the midst of the corn fields and was visited only by a few old hags in greasy buckskins, who came to hoe the weeds from their growing crops. The resort of the men was on the prairie near the village. He could hear their shouting and see, in the distance, their games and horse-races, but no one came near him.

The village itself was in plain view from where he lay. A steep bluff thrust its rocky bulk out into the water, making a sharp angle round which the river turned. On top of the promontory, on a level spot fifty or sixty feet above the water, within a bastioned palisade, stood the huddled, smoking lodges of the Mandans, looking like giant molehills. Here and there tall poles reared their tops high above the lodges, and drying scaffolds, like great gridirons on edge, relieved the undulating skyline with their perpendicular lines. To the right, on the level prairie near the village, rose the rigid burial scaffolds. To the left swept the smooth breadth of the river, with its lofty bluffs and broken tablelands beyond stretching away to the blue distance. Now and then a tilted bull-boat moved across the river, or a horseman passed over the prairie, his right arm moving up and down regularly as the horse's feet, as he beat the animal with his quirt. There was no other movement.

At sunset, Whirlwind saw the Mandans driving in their ponies towards the village. The lodge tops smoked more actively, and when the heat lifted and the cool night air began to blow from the river, Whirlwind heard the steady beat of tom-toms, mingled with snatches of song and the wild, wolf like yelps of the dancers. When the moon rose, he made ready to enter the village.

It was obvious that no one could easily get into the town from the river side. The hill was too steep. Nor did he think it wise to walk up the long path, where he might be met and discovered long before he reached the town. Instead, he left the river, went back to the high prairie, and turned towards the village from that side. As he went, he noticed the bunchgrass was just knee high.

Advancing, he found himself in the midst of the burial ground. On every side tall scaffolds had been erected, and on these, wrapped in buffalo robes, high out of reach of animals and men, reposed the Mandan dead. These grim sepulchres reared their gaunt frames, silent and rigid against the moon, breathing a most unwholesome odor. Here and there, tall and lonely upon long poles, hung tattered scarecrows made of boughs and skins, swaying in the wind, offerings to the Master of Life. Whirlwind hurried through this desolate place, scaring the

ravens which perched upon the scaffolds and
flapped away with hoarse cries as he approached.
Not far off he saw the place of weeping, where two
dozen human skulls sat grinning in a ghastly ring.

He made haste to escape from this city of the
dead, and approached the village, from which the
sounds of the dancing came louder and louder. He
found it defended by a palisade of logs about a foot
in thickness and eighteen feet high, having a trench
inside in which the warriors could lie and fire between the upright logs, if an enemy, attacked the
town. The palisade had become much dilapidated
through lapse of years, and there was no lack of
openings in its sagging walls large enough to admit
a man. Whirlwind slipped through one in the
shadow of a wattled bastion, crossed the shallow
trench, and found himself within the village.

The lodges of the Mandans stood huddled together without any order or arrangement. There
was scarcely room to pass between them. They
were large dwellings, forty to sixty feet in diameter,
roughly circular in shape and rising to a height of
some twenty feet in the middle, with low, massive
walls and sloping roofs covered thick with beaten
clay. Their unsymmetrical shapes, spotted with
patches of ragged weeds and rusty grass, made
them look like natural hillocks, but the smoke
curling from their tops gave the lie to the resemblance. Upon the roofs lay buffalo skulls, bull-boats,
sledges, baskets, pottery, and every variety of
household utensil. Here and there among the

lodges, wherever space permitted, stood great double-decked scaffolds upon which meat and Indian corn were drying. Through this maze of moundlike lodges Whirlwind moved cautiously, muffled in his robe, lance in hand. No one noticed him, for all were intent on the dance going forward in the central plaza of the village, where the warriors of the Buffalo Band were celebrating their prowess after the custom of their Order. The people crowded all the passages, blocking them completely. Many stood upon the broad walls of the lodges, or sat upon the sloping roofs, covering the whole structure from eaves to smoke-hole in their anxiety to get a good view of the dance. Whirlwind, finding it impossible to proceed on the ground, climbed upon one of the housetops, and looking over the shoulders of those in front, saw all that was going on.

In the middle of the village was a great space of level ground upon which all the nearest lodges fronted, the white, weathered logs of their projecting doorways contrasting sharply in the moonlight with the dark earthen walls. Opposite Whirlwind, across the plaza, a number of tall poles swayed in the wind, bearing hideous effigies with trailing garments and grinning, blackened faces, dominating the closed entrance to the great medicine lodge. In the midst of the open space stood an upright cylinder of planks six or eight feet high encircled by vines and withes, looking like a headless hogshead. This ark, or "Big Canoe of the First Man," as the

Mandans called it, was the center of all their most sacred ceremonies, the memorial of the escape of their first ancestor from the great flood.

Around this ark the naked dancers stamped and circled, shouting their war cries, brandishing war-clubs, shields, and lances, bending and leaping with the wild enthusiasm of the celebration. All were painted with the marks of their prowess in war. Every man wore a buffalo tail at his belt behind and the forelock and horns of a buffalo upon his head, as the badge of his Order. To one side stood the drummers thumping the tom-toms in unison and singing lustily, while the sponsor of the society, a woman dressed in a white leather smock, her face anointed with vermilion, passed to and fro at intervals, offering a bowl of water to the leaders of the dance.

These were two in number, and carried shields, and lances feathered to resemble gigantic arrows and decorated with tassels of dyed horsehair. On their heads they wore ferocious masks made of the entire skin of the head of a buffalo, with horns complete. These men were pledged never to retreat, but to fight as stubbornly as a mad bull. They moved about on the outskirts of the dance, bellowing and stamping in imitation of the buffalo, and keeping mimic guard over the herd of dancers.

As the dance went on, the spectators joined in the uproar, singing and shouting and firing their guns in the air from the housetops. Such a celebration broke the monotony of their sedentary lives, and all took keen delight in the movement and color of the spectacle. No one paid the least attention to Whirlwind, who began to push his way through the crowd, jostling the people in order to count the coups and looking searchingly into the face of every man whose figure even faintly resembled Killer's. Muffled in his robe, with only his eyes showing, he passed completely round the plaza without finding his enemy. Every man in the village was there, and the Mandans were a small people, decimated by war and smallpox, who scarcely numbered 250 warriors all told. But Whirlwind could not find his man.

He took his stand out of the way in the shadow cast by a projecting entry, and kept his eye upon A-nu'tah, who stood near, watching the dance. He thought she looked sad; maybe she was not happy with Killer the Mandan after all. He did not care. When the dance at length broke up, and people began to go into their lodges for the night, Whirlwind saw the woman walk into the very lodgedoor near which he stood. Presently one of the leaders of the dance went in after her, still wearing his buffalo mask. As he entered the passage leading down into the lodge, he removed the mask, and Whirlwind rejoiced. It was Killer! He had found his man!

When the plaza was deserted, Whirlwind turned to the lodge of his enemy. A log deeply notched into rough steps leaned against the earth wall. He climbed up this primitive ladder, walked out upon the sloping roof, and crept up to the smoke-hole.

The opening was about four feet square, and covered by a loosely woven, inverted basket of bent willow sticks. In wet weather an old robe was thrown over this light framework to keep the rain from getting into the lodge. Whirlwind lay down and looked through the smoke-hole, covering his head with the edge of his robe so that its outline could not be seen against the stars from below.

The lodge was spacious and lofty, with a clean-swept floor of hard clay and four great pillars bearing up the sloping, smoke-stained roof. In the center, immediately below the smoke-hole, was the fireplace—a circular depression curbed with stone, over which a kettle hung from a tripod. About the fireplace lay scattered earthen pots, a mortar and pestle for grinding corn, bowls, spoons, and other household utensils. Round the low walls at regular intervals stout posts supported the cross beams upon which the lower ends of the rafters rested, and against which the sloping timbers of the walls reclined with all their heavy load of earth. All round the room between these posts were placed the handsome curtained beds of the family. Near the door, on stages out of reach of the dogs, were piled together all manner of objects—parfleches, baskets of corn, sledges, bull-boats, snowshoes, harness, hides, and stiff slabs of sun-dried meat.

A screen of rough planks stood between the fireplace and the door, shielding the fire from drafts. Across this hung a painted buffalo robe, and against it, next the fire, was a low lounge neatly made of mats of peeled willow rods. On this sat Killer, smoking his long pipe, the otter-skin tobacco pouch across his knees. Around the fire were gathered his relatives, who shared the roomy lodge with him—his brother, his nephew, a dozen women and children, all eating, chattering and laughing together. One of the women placed fresh fuel on the fire, laying the sticks crosswise one upon another, and soon the lodge was lighted brightly and the smoke brought tears to Whirlwind's smarting eyes. Still he lay watching patiently as one by one the sleepy Mandans left the fire and retired to the beds around the walls. Last of all Killer laid aside his pipe, weary with the exertion of the dance. He went to his bed in the place of honor and lay down beside his wife, drawing his buffalo robe around him.

When all had grown quiet, Whirlwind sat up and looked over the village. There was not a sound. The Mandans, not being a nomadic people, had very few dogs. The only stir was among the ponies picketed nearby. The moundlike lodges, dingy and formless without, smoked faintly here and there. But no one was abroad. The moonlight flooded the plaza with its gruesome effigies, picked out the tall scaffolds and tottering palisade with sharp black shadows, and softened the harsh outlines of the dismal city of the dead beyond. Downstream, where the river swung towards the southwest, the low moon danced and shimmered on the moving waters.

Whirlwind descended from the lodge roof and

stepped down into the doorway, pushing aside the curtain of skin which hung there. Muffled in his robe, he walked boldly into the light of the dying fire and sat on the couch beside it. There was meat in the kettle simmering above the embers. So Whirlwind took the spoon of ram's-horn lying there, and helped himself. He was almost famished by his long journey. Often he had been afraid to build a fire, and had eaten his meat raw, when he had had any at all to eat. Now, as he ate, he felt his strength return to him, for the warm stew was good.

Killer was asleep on his bed in the place of honor. But A-nu'tah his wife was still awake. She had seen Whirlwind come into the lodge, muffled in his robe, and could not tell who he was. So she touched her husband and waked him and whispered, "Who is that fellow by the fire? Get up and see what he wants!"

But Killer was weary with dancing all night. It was the custom for a hungry man to enter any lodge and eat, if food was ready. So he said to his wife, "Never mind. Let him eat. Perhaps he is hungry." Then he turned to his sleep again. But A-nu'tah could not tell who the man was, for the fire was very low. She lay quiet and watched him.

Killer had left his pipe and tobacco pouch beside the fire. When Whirlwind had eaten his fill, he took tobacco from the pouch and filled the pipe. He lighted it with a coal from the fire, and leaned back at east against the mat at the head of the willow bed. He had had no tobacco for a long time, and this was very good. He drew long inhalations, blowing the smoke upwards with whispered prayers to White Man Above for success in this undertaking.

A-nu'tah was still awake. She had a premonition that something unpleasant was about to happen. She roused her sleeping husband and said, "Look! Who is this man smoking your pipe in the lodge? Get up and see what he wants, for he has satisfied his hunger."

Then Killer was angry with his wife for disturbing him. He was a leader of the Buffalo Band, and kept open house to all comers. He would not get up, and threatened his wife with a quirting if she disturbed him again. He turned to sleep once more. And after a time A-nu'tah dozed also.

When the pipe was smoked out, Whirlwind screened his face, and turning on his elbow, with his toe pushed a stick across the embers of the fire. Soon a little flame sprang up, lighting the great, sombre room with a bright, uncertain light. No one stirred in the stiff, boxlike beds around the walls.

The bed of Killer stood at the back of the room in the place of honor, with its curtains of soft, fringed elk-skin about it. At the head of the bed, on wooden pegs let into the post there, hung his shield and quiver, his warbonnet in its painted case, his lance and medicine bundle. Topping all these, the grotesque buffalo mask he had worn in the dance that night leered down at him ferociously, as though the spirit of the dead buffalo mocked the insecure slumbers of its slayer. But Killer slept on, unmindful of ghosts and men, his naked chest rising and falling evenly above the edge of his buffalo robe.

The robe hung from the side of his bed to the floor. Upon its white surface were painted in gay colors the warlike exploits of the Mandan, showing his wounds, his victims, the prisoners and arms and horses he had taken, his own figure dominant and victorious in every group. The Mandan men excelled all others in this graphic art, and Killer was a master among his fellows. Others might outline pony tracks and flying arrows, but their drawings of men and horses were crude and childish. *His* had life. As the flame flashed its bright, flickering light upon the painted figures, they seemed to Whirlwind to move of themselves, re-enacting the fearful scenes in which they had lost their lives.

Whirlwind got up and approached the bed. As he did so, he saw upon the robe the painted representation of a boy with a bull's head upon his shield, lying thrust through with a lance.

With all his might the Cheyenne chief drove the lance that had killed his son into the body of the sleeping Mandan. Killer made no outcry, but moved convulsively, and his body rolled with a heavy thud upon the earthen floor, while A-nu'tah, suddenly awakened, cowered beneath her robe upon the bed.

In a moment Whirlwind had removed the scalp, and giving his war cry, rushed out of the lodge.

Behind him he could hear the wailing of the

women, the tumult and confusion as the villagers ran from their lodges to learn what had happened, the firing of guns and shouting of the war whoop. But Whirlwind slipped through a gap in the palisade, clambered down the steep bank to the river, and finding a bull-boat, climbed in, pushed off, and drifted away down the swift current of the mighty Missouri, leaving the Mandans to mourn their dead without even a trace or a trail to follow when it should grow light. Soon he had drifted out of hearing, and was alone with the moon, the river, and the ghostly, boundless plains.

Whirlwind's mind was at rest. His heart was good. He had succeeded. The medicine of the Thunder was strong! He could go home now and bury his son in peace. The women would raise a lofty scaffold on the prairie and lay the long bundle upon it. He would kill his son's pony beneath the

scaffold, in order that the boy might not go afoot into the spirit land. All things would be done properly at last. The women would wail and gash themselves. He and his relatives would give away their ponies and cut their hair in mourning for their kinsman. For the spirit of the boy whose body rested upon the lonely scaffold would not be lonely now. Little Chief would not go unattended to the Happy Hunting Grounds.

GLOSSARY

Buffalo Chips—The sun-dried excrement of the buffalo, used for fuel where wood was scarce.

Calumet (cal'u-met)—The long stem of the pipe of peace used in the Calumet Dance. When an Indian smoked, he was making a burnt offering to his gods, and believed that the fragrant smoke carried his words up to them. For this reason, whatever he said when smoking was sure to be true, and Indians always smoked when making serious agreements of any kind, such as treaties and oaths.

Catlinite (cat'lin-ite)—The red stone used in making Indian pipe bowls and obtained only in the pipestone quarry in Minnesota. Named after the famous Indian painter Catlin.

Coup (*pr.* coo)—The French word for a blow, used to mean the striking of an enemy (by an Indian warrior) with the hand or something held in the hand. So to touch or strike an enemy was the highest honor to be obtained in war; killing and scalping were regarded as less dangerous, and so less honorable. To touch an enemy was called counting *coup*, and the same term was applied to the practice of warriors enumerating coups already struck.

Pemmican (pem'mi-can)—A very nourishing food made of dried meat, tallow, and cherries pounded up and dried. A small amount would feed a man for days. It tasted good, and was called the Indian's bread-and-butter. It would keep indefinitely, if dry.

Tabus (ta-bus')—This word, sometimes spelled *taboos*, refers to the prohibitions and obligations of primitive religion. For instance, it was tabu for Ironshirt to eat food with an iron implement. If he broke this rule, his iron shirt would no longer protect him, it was believed.

Tipi (ti'pi)—This word, sometimes spelled *tepee*, is a Sioux word meaning dwelling of leather, or skin tent, and refers always to the conical shelter of buffalo or horse hides used by the Plains Indians. A wigwam or wickiup is not a tipi.

Travois (tra'vois)—The French word, meaning "drag," applied to the vehicle of dragging poles used by the Plains Indians. It was made by crossing the small ends of two tipi poles at the withers of the horse, letting the big ends drag the ground behind, one on either side. Across the poles, behind the horse, a basket or network was fastened on which to carry packs or people.

Sun Dance—Sometimes called Medicine Lodge, was the principal dance or religious ceremony of the Plains Indians. It lasted for several days, and the whole tribe attended. Sometimes warriors tortured themselves during the dance, in the hope of winning the favor of their savage gods on the warpath.

NOTES

Note 1. Indian Songs. Writers on Indian subjects have seldom given a fair share of their space to Indian music. The Plains tribes were fond of singing, and music accompanied almost every activity of their lives. The songs were suggestive rather than explanatory, and usually contained few words. Most of our own songs contain only one inspired phrase embedded in a mass of prosaic terminology and explanation. We remember the inspired phrase—"Nearer my God, to Thee," or "For auld Lang syne"—but we soon forget the padding. The Indian community was so small that the singer could safely omit all the padding and give merely the central idea, the inspired phrase, in a few words, knowing that his hearers would understand the surrounding circumstances, or perhaps not much caring whether they understood or not. He filled out the melody with meaningless vocables. Hence the sharp, poetic abruptness of Indian songs, which go to the heart of the matter with all the directness of an old English ballad.

Happy Hunting Grounds

For the words of most of the Indian songs here given, I am indebted to the late George Bent, of Colony, Oklahoma, a Cheyenne himself, and probably better informed than any other regarding his people's history. However, a number of songs have been adapted from those recorded by the Bureau of American Ethnology in different publications, as follows:

Chapter 4. Calumet Song of Counsel, *B.A.E. 22nd Annual Report*, Fletcher, "The Hako," page 101.

Chapter 5. War Song of Little Chief, *B.A.E. 27th Annual Report*, Fletcher, "The Omaha Tribe," page 429.

Chapter 6. Song of the Strong Hearts, *B.A.E. Bul. 61*, Densmore, "Teton Sioux Music," page 322.

Chapter 6. Whirlwind's War Song, *B.A.E. 17th Annual Report*, Mooney, "Calendar History of the Kiowa Indians," page 329.

Note 2. Thunder Bird. "Thunder and lightning were usually supposed to be produced by a being or a number of beings different from all others. On the great plains, where the phenomena of thunderstorms are very striking . . . they were supposed to be caused by birds of enormous size, which produced thunder by flapping their wings and the lightning by opening and closing their eyes. The great downpour which generally accompanies thunder was often accounted for by supposing that the bird carries a lake of fresh water on its back. The Mandan supposed that it was because the thunder bird broke through the clouds, the bottom of the skyey reservoir. . . . Sometimes one thunder bird is spoken of, and sometimes a family of them, or else several adults of different colors." (*B.A.E. Bul. 30*, part 2, pages 746–47.)

Note 3. Medicine. "We have no one word which can convey the meaning of 'Medicine' as used by the Indians. Sometimes it shadows forth holiness, mystery, spirits, luck, visions, dreams, prophecies, at others the concealed and obscure forces of nature, which work for us good or evil. . . . If success crowns their efforts, their medicine was *good*; and defeat, suffering, death, are all the legitimate fruits of *bad* medicine. . . . Their faith in their medicine to secure their personal protection from physical harm,

Notes

as well as to promote their general welfare, is simply marvellous."
(Clark, *Indian Sign Language*, page 248.)

Note 4. The Face of Na'pi. White visitors to Glacier National
Park will perhaps look in vain for a resemblance between the
patch of snow on the summit of Going-to-the-Sun Mountain and
a human face, as seen from Going-to-the-Sun Camp. This resemblance is noticed by the white man only when the peak is viewed
from certain points on the southern shore of St. Mary's Lake,
where it is very striking. But for the Indians this gleaming snow-
field represented the face of the Blackfoot culture hero, no
matter from what point they viewed it.

Note 5. Sign Language. "As commonly known, the sign language belongs to the tribes between the Missouri and the Rocky
Mountains, and from Fraser River, British Columbia, to the Rio
Grande. . . . In this great treeless area of the plains, stretching
nearly 2,000 miles from north to south, and occupied by tribes of
many different stocks, all constantly shifting about in pursuit of
the buffalo herds and thus continually brought into friendly meeting or hostile collision, the necessities of nomadic life resulted in
the evolution of a highly developed system of gesture communication which, for all ordinary purposes, hardly fell short of the
perfection of a spoken language. . . . It may . . . be described as
a motional equivalent of the Indian pictograph, the conventional
sign being usually a close reference to the predominant character-
istic of the object in shape, habit, or purpose. The signs are made
almost entirely with the hands, either one or both. Minor differences exist, like dialects in spoken languages, the differences
being naturally greatest at the two extremes of the sign-language
area, but even with these slight dissimilarities a Sioux or a Blackfoot from the upper Missouri has no difficulty in communicating
with a visiting Kiowa or Comanche from the Texas border on
any subject from the negotiating of a treaty to the recital of a
mythic story or the telling of a hunting incident. The claim of
any particular tribe to having invented the system may be set
down as mere boasting, but it is universally admitted that the
Crows, Cheyenne, and Kiowa are most expert in its use. . . . In
fluent grace of movement a conversation in the sign language

between a Cheyenne and a Kiowa is the very poetry of motion."
(*B.A.E. Bul. 30*, page 567.)

Note 6. Calumet. "The calumet was employed by ambassadors and travelers as a passport; it was used in ceremonies designed to conciliate foreign and hostile nations and to conclude lasting peace; to ratify the alliance of friendly tribes; to secure favorable weather for journeys; to bring needed rain; and to attest contracts and treaties which could not be violated without incurring the wrath of the gods . . . the Omaha and cognate names for this dance signify 'to make a sacred kinship.' . . . The one for whom the dance for the calumet was performed became thereafter the adopted son of the performer. From Dorsey's account of the . . . calumets, it is evident that they are together the most highly organized emblems known to religious observances anywhere, and it is further in evidence that the pipe is an accessory rather than the dominant or chief object in this highly complex synthetic symbol of the source, reproduction, and conservation of life . . . if the calumet is offered and accepted it is the custom to smoke . . . and the engagements contracted are held sacred and inviolable. . . . The Indians profess that the violation of such an engagement never escapes just punishment. In the heat of battle, if an adversary offer the calumet to his opponent and he accept it, the weapons on both sides are at once laid down; but to accept or to refuse the offer of the calumet is optional. There are caluments for various kinds of public engagements, and when such bargains are made an exchange of calumets is usual, in this manner rendering the contract or bargain sacred. . . . The use of the calumet, sometimes called 'Peace-pipe' . . . was wide-spread in the Mississippi Valley generally. It has been found among the Potawotami, Cheyenne, Shoshoni, Pawnee Loups, Piegan, Santee, Yanktonais, Sihasapa, Kansa, Siksika, Crows, Cree, Skitswish, Nez Percés, Illinois, Chickasaw, Choctaw, Chitimacha, Chippewa, Winnebago, and Natchez." (*B.A.E. Bul. 30*, part 1, page 192ff.)

Note 7. Preservation of Bones. The practice of preserving the bones of the deceased was almost universal among the inhabitants of both North and South America, though perhaps observed more among tribes of sedentary habit. However, a number of instances within historic times may be cited among the nomadic tribes, such as that recorded by Mooney of the Kiowa chief, Sitting Bear, who in 1870 brought the bones of his slain son all the way from Texas to place them in a tipi, where he kept them until his own death a year later. (*B.A.E. 17th Annual Report*, "Calendar History of the Kiowa," page 327.)

"The opinion underlying all these customs was, that a part of the soul, or one of the souls, dwelt in the bones. . . . The traveler on our western prairies often notices the buffalo skulls, countless numbers of which bleach on those vast plains, arranged in circles and symmetrical piles by the careful hands of the native hunters. The explanation they offer for this custom gives the key to the whole theory and practice of preserving the osseous relics of the dead, as well human as brute. They say that 'the bones contain the spirits of the slain animals, and that some time in the future they will rise from the earth, re-clothe themselves with flesh, and stock the prairies anew.' . . . The Indian thought that the soul now enjoying the delights of the happy hunting grounds would some time return to the bones, take on flesh, and live again." (Daniel G. Brinton, in *The Myths of the New World*.)

Note 8. Dog Soldiers. The principal Warrior Order, or Society of Warriors among the Cheyennes. There were four such orders, each with its own uniform, leaders, and ways of doing things. Whenever possible, society members went to war in a body. They were fraternal, religious, warlike societies. They took their name from the mythical watchdogs who were said to have given them their uniform, dances, etc. Only four of the Dog Soldiers wore sashes like Whirlwind's. These four never retreated.